BLO

JANE BLONDE

TWICE THE SPYLET

JILL MARSHALL

JANE BLONDE

Twice the Spylet

Jill Marshall

Jill Marshall Books

First published by Macmillan Children's Books 2007

Copyright © Jill Marshall

A CIP catalogue record for this book is available from the National Library of New Zealand

ISBN 978-1-99-002415-3 Paperback

Cover Design by Katie Gannon

Illustrations by Madison Fotti-Knowles

For Christine, Gary and Leigh, with love x

Chapter 1 Spy cleaning

Jane Blonde, Sensational Spylet, stepped out of the car wash and looked around her. Her slick black Ultra-Gog glasses penetrated the shadows circling Abe 'n' Jean's Clean Machines (MAKE YOUR CAR A STAR!). Somewhere out there, G-Mamma her SPI:KE (Solomon's Polifications: Kid Educator), was posing an enemy for her to thwart. It was no longer enough simply to try to get out of harm's way. Two missions in which she'd barely skirted death had taught them that. Jane Blonde had to learn to get ready. Be on the offensive. Fight.

Of course, it helped that this was no ordinary car wash. It had been set up by her father, super-SPI Boz "Brilliance" Brown, when he'd used his amazing Crystal Clarification Process to transform himself into another human being: Abe Rownigan. He'd then gone into business with Janey's mother, his wife, former super-SPI Gina Bellarina, who had been brain-wiped for her own safety and now led a simple life as Jean Brown, mother of one Janey Brown and cleaner extraordinaire.

Mrs Brown had no idea that the car wash was actually an enormous Wower – a spy shower into which a girl had stepped earlier, a girl with fine mousy hair and scabby knees like knots in string. Janey had giggled as angled jets of steam darted across her, enveloping her in glistening,

1

transformational droplets. Unlike the Wower of G-Mamma's Spylab, which just two robotic hands to impregnate her hair with a platinum gleam and coax it into a sleek multifunction ponytail, this Wower-with-knobs-on had eight – enough to work on the largest saloon car. In no time at all she had been scrubbed of her ordinariness, wrapped in air-light, air-tight silver Lycra, and buffeted into shiny Jane Blonde fabulousness complete with the most bouffant, bouncy topknot of a ponytail she had ever had.

G-Mamma's voice hissed from the SPI Visualator around Janey's neck. 'Remember – look for their Achilles heel.'

'What was that again?' whispered Janey. Despite the powerful certainty that coursed through her whenever she had Wowed into Jane Blonde, she was still a tiny bit nervous of what lay ahead. The most adventurous thing she'd done in the last few weeks was school crossing patrol, but now that school was over for the Easter holidays, G-Mamma was insistent that her spy training should be ramped up.

'Their weakness, Blondette. Use your strength against their weakness. Bogies, two o'clock.'

Janey took a moment to realise that G-Mamma wasn't being disgusting, and she spun around to her right. The enemy was approaching, racing at her with long blonde hair streaming out behind her and a Fur- Real Pet dachshund yapping at her heels.

'Ariel!' It was Janey's first enemy – or rather, someone pretending to be Janey's first enemy.

Ariel was nearly upon her, and Janey found herself staring down the barrel of a small bronze pistol. 'OK, Blonde,' she said under her breath. 'Go to it.'

She banged both feet down hard against the ground and the Fleet-feet she wore on her feet propelled her right over Ariel's head. She knew she had to turn herself into a moving target – much more difficult to hit than a fixed one – and make sure that her face, the only bit of her that wasn't protected by her bullet-proof SPIsuit, was out of harm's way. Ariel spun round with the gun waving madly in Janey's direction, and Janey knew she had her. Ariel wasn't strong. She was little and wiry and devious, but not as power packed as Janey. Taking her by surprise, Janey stopped abruptly, took a quick step backwards, so that Ariel cannoned into her with her arm still extended and ow trapped under Janey's armpit, and wrenched the gun out of Ariel's hand. She whipped around, trained the pistol on the enemy's face, and pulled off the long, blonde wig to reveal G-Mamma's boingy curls and beaming smile. 'My turn with the gun, Goldilocks,' she said with a grin.

'Good, Blonde-girl,' squeaked G-Mamma, trying to imitate Ariel's high-pitched voice. 'Now get the gun out of my face, run once around the car wash, and I'll be ready for you when you're back.'

Janey took off around the shed from which she'd emerged only moments earlier. She threw her head back to the sky as she Fleet-footed around the car wash, as wild and free and lightning-fast as a cheetah.

In no time she was back at the front of the car wash. 'What now?' she wondered. Her last real enemy had been another girl, Paulette Soleil, who had turned out to be the half-sister of her best friend and fellow Spylet Alfie Halliday, aka Al Halo. Maybe it would be the French girl, but Janey knew better than to make assumptions. There was a scrabbling sound from the bushes; Janey braced herself for what was coming next. It was the rat-dog – or rather, G-Mamma on all fours gnashing her teeth, with Trouble on her head yowling like a werewolf and snapping his head back and forth. He'd seen the rat-dog at very close quarters so knew exactly what to do.

'Easy,' breathed Janey. The enemy didn't like water; that much she knew. She couldn't get to the hosepipes before big rat-dog was upon her, but she had a water substitute. With her left hand tightly gripping her Girl-gauntleted right hand, she crouched down, forward rolled until she was directly before the fake beast, then slashed across G-Mamma's sleeve with the pen nib that she'd forced out of her Girl-Gauntlet glove and squeezed with all her might. Midnight-blue ink squirted all over G-Mamma's arm, and as the SPI: KE turned to stare in horror at the disastrous stain on her fuchsia pink SPIsuit, Janey forward rolled again, planted a foot into the shoulder of both SPI:KE and Spycat, and shoved them asunder.

'Brilliant, brilliant. Cost me a SPIsuit, girly-girl, but you can make it up to me in Easter eggs.' G-Mamma brushed herself down and checked that Trouble was OK. He was purring like a tractor. 'Not had so much fun in ages, have you, Twubs? Right. Off around the block, Blonde, and back here in thirty seconds.'

And so they went on, Jane Blonde fighting off pretend enemies old and new with a mixture of gymnastic grace and good old gadgets – even using her gleaming ponytail to dangle Trouble over the car wash when she guessed that an enemy's weakness was that he didn't like heights. In seconds she had knotted her hair through his collar, shot up the side of the building on her ASPIC hoverboard (Aeronautical SPI Conveyor), used the grip of her Girl-gauntlet to climb up the metal chimney stack, and whisked Trouble into the chimney with a flick of her head so that there was only thirty feet of blackness below him.

'Sorry, Trouble,' she said a moment later, cuddling him close as she clambered back down to G-Mamma. 'Don't you fuss over him,' said the SPI:KE. 'He's quite happy to do it, and anyway, you never know when you might have to fight one of your friends.' Janey shook her head. 'I could never do that, G-Mamma.'

'Well, just remember how many of your enemies have tried to be your friend at some stage.' What G- Mamma said was true. Both Ariel and Paulette had befriended Janey as a way of getting what they wanted. 'Achilles heel. Remember that.'

5

Janey thought about that, all the way home in the Clean-Jean van that G-Mamma had "borrowed" for the occasion. She relied on her friends a lot. It had taken her a long time to find them – G-Mamma, Trouble, Alfie and his mother (who was either headmistress Maisie Halliday or super-SPI Halo, depending on what was going on) and the very best new friend of all, her dad: Boz Brilliance Brown aka Solomon Brown aka Abe Rownigan. She sighed. Where was he now? And when would he get in touch with her again?

'It's dawn.' G-Mamma pointed at the pink sky illuminating the city. 'Just time to de-Wow and do a bit more training before that mother of yours wakes up.'

Janey nodded, holding back a yawn. She was pretty tired, but there was no way she would escape G-Mamma in this kind of mood. Furthermore, she had to do whatever she could to get along with her SPI:Kid Educator right now. Janey had only just been forgiven for nearly blowing the whole of their spy organisation, Solomon's Polifical Investigations, wide open: she'd hung on to a piece of LipSPICK (the ruler-like Lip-activated SPI-Camera Kilobank that allowed video footage to be transferred to any location, given the right lip-print), which brought an image of her father to life, just for a moment or two, every time she gave it a tiny kiss. Unfortunately Copernicus – SPI's most sinister enemy – had seen it too. Now her father had been forced into hiding again, her mother had been re-brain-wiped so she didn't remember anything much about her husband, and Janey had to tread very carefully around G-Mamma.

'OK,' she said reluctantly as they climbed the spiral staircase to G-Mamma's Spylab. 'Just for an hour though. Then I really do need to clean up my room. I was supposed to do it last night.'

G-Mamma pulled a face. 'Cleaning? Euw. Well, don't expect me to help you with that! Although . . . hmmm, yippy yes yo-yos. It seems like as good a time as any to spy-proof your room. Go on, girly-girl, let's clean!'

For the next forty minutes, Janey put away her stray books, righted and polished her mirror, vacuumed furiously, and returned all her puzzle books and other SPI-buys – gadgets she'd received as presents over the years – to the box under her bed in which she stored these treasures. 'G-Mamma,' she said eventually, 'what has this got to do with spying? And why are you sitting there watching?'

'You missed a bit.' G-Mamma sniffed, licking icing sugar off her fingers from the doughnut she'd been sure to bring with her. 'And for your information, I am not watching, I am *SPI:king.* We'll be able to lay traps only when you know exactly where everything is, and that everything is spanky clean and sparkly. That'll do. Now,' she said as she jumped off the bed, 'back to that mirror.'

As they stood before the dressing table G-Mamma licked the end of her little finger and drew a short line across the surface of the glass.

'I just polished that!' said Janey.

'Watch and learn, Zany Janey. Watch and learn.'

The track of saliva on the mirror had completely disappeared. Janey looked at it and shrugged. What did that prove? But then G-Mamma leaned forward and blew gently on her reflection. A puff of condensation clouded the mirror, and right across the polished surface was a clear finger-width line.

'You see?' G-Mamma stood back to let the mist clear, then did it again.

'Right, I get that now. If someone comes in and breathes on the mirror, I'll be able to see it.'

'Yes! Or you can leave an invisible message for me to pick up. Good. Now, what else?' G-Mamma rummaged around in her capacious bib pocket and pulled out a large container of baby powder. 'Don't worry, it's not for your biddy botty. Tell me, what did you touch last?'

'Erm, the book shelf,' said Janey.

'All righty.' Crossing over to the book shelf, G-Mamma sprinkled talcum powder over the surface of the last book Janey had popped on top of its pile. 'See?'

'Good idea, fingerprints!' Janey could hardly believe it.

G-Mamma nodded. 'You go and lift them off with sticky tape and stick them on dark paper so you can see them properly. And keep them as a record of your fingerprints, so you'll know which are somebody else's.'

'I know,' said Janey.

Now she was on the case. She followed G-Mamma around, fascinated, as the SPI:KE opened a drawer slightly and drew a pencil line on its side to mark its position so Janey could tell if anyone moved it, then drew another faint line down the side of the stack of homework books on Janey's desk for the same purpose. Finally, G-Mamma leaned over to Janey's head and yanked out a couple of her pale brown hairs. 'Ow! You could have warned me.'

'What's the spy motto, Blondette? Surprise, surprise, surprise. Now stop whingeing and get busy.' Once again G-Mamma licked the end of her finger, but this time she used it to moisten the ends of the hairs she'd plucked from Janey's head and stuck one across the window frame and the other across the lid of Janey's SPI-buys box. 'Invisible to everyone else, but if you come back in and those hairs are broken or missing, we'll know someone's been in here.'

'G-Mamma, that's brilliant!' Janey was amazed. She'd learned about this stuff, but it was great to be putting into practice to spy-proof her room. 'It's like . . . proper spying.'

'You don't say, Blondette,' said G-Mamma, looking rather hurt. 'I am a proper spy, you know, not just a glamour queen. Oh heck, there's your mother.' She headed for the tunnel as Jean Brown called up the stairs. 'Don't forget to buy me an Easter egg while you're out.'

G-Mamma's voice became muffled as she went further down the tunnel, and Janey grinned as her SPI:

KE's hippopotamus behind disappeared from view. As soon as the panel at the back of the fireplace had slid shut, Janey ran out of her bedroom and down the stairs.

Her mother was standing by the door with a parcel in her hand. 'This is funny. I didn't think they delivered the post on Good Friday. Anyway, it's addressed to you. Think it might be from . . . you know . . .'

'From Abe?' Janey grabbed the parcel, shot down the hall and into the kitchen. The box was very similar to the one in which Janey stored her precious SPI-buys. Maybe it was another gadget! She ripped off the lid and rummaged around for a moment.

'Oh, Janey, they're great! Perfect for the summer. And just your size,' said her mum over her shoulder.

'They're weird.' Janey held up a pair of shoes – light summery sandals made from pale blue cloth, with long cotton straps that crossed around the ankle and up the leg. They didn't look at all practical for running in, or doing anything else in for that matter. She couldn't imagine why her father, who knew better than anyone that spying could be physically challenging, would send something so impractical.

'They're not weird,' said Jean, foraging around in the bottom of the box. 'They're espadrilles. Summer shoes. It's probably a bit cold for them just at the moment, but you can put them away for a couple of months. Look, there's even directions on how to put them on!'

She held up a little piece of paper. It certainly was headed 'Directions', with a picture of the sandals beneath it, but apart from that all there was on the paper scrap was a diagram of a compass with the S circled in pencil. 'Well, that's not much use,' said Jean Brown. 'Never mind though. I used to have some when I was younger. It's just like lacing up ballet shoes. It's funny he didn't send a note or anything.'

Janey nodded. There wasn't much she could say really. Jean wasn't to know that Abe wished dearly to be with his family again but couldn't risk putting them in danger. And anyway, he *had* sent a note, saying 'Directions', along with a southerly compass point. She just didn't yet know what it meant.

'I'll just go and put them away,' she said, replacing the lid on the box, 'and then we can go and do those errands you wanted. My room's all clean.'

Her mother leaned over and gave her a kiss on the forehead. 'Good girl. That sounds like a plan. Maybe we can go for lunch somewhere.'

'Yeah, great,' said Janey.

She went quietly to her bedroom, wondering what the note meant. He was obviously somewhere south. But south of where? South London? South Pacific? It was still a mystery. Bending down, Janey shuffled the box in beside its twin that held her SPI-buys, smiling at the two boxes of Dad-related goodies.

It was only then that she noticed something.

11

The hair that G-Mamma had stuck across the SPI-buys box just half an hour before was missing.

Janey's gut churned. Her spy instincts were suddenly all a-quiver, ready to alert her to danger. She'd just heard from her dad, only minutes ago. And already, someone had been in her room – possibly trying to track down new information about Abe's whereabouts. Whenever someone was looking for her father, the problems began. She would have to warn him somehow, get in touch and let him know that he might be in danger, that she and her mother and the other spies might also be at risk once again.

And unable to help herself, Janey suddenly grinned. Maybe the Easter break was not going to be as dull as she had predicted. In fact, it could be quite the opposite. Jane Blonde's next mission was about to begin.

Chapter 2 Two-way mirrors

It's gone! The hair on my box of SPI-buys has disappeared,' cried Janey, scooting into the Spylab on her ASPIC.

G-Mamma looked down at her, puzzled, from the cabinet in which she was stowing the talcum powder. 'What, already?'

Raising one eyebrow sceptically, G-Mamma headed back through the tunnel to Janey's room. Janey popped through behind her, still crouching on the ASPIC. 'You see?' she said. 'Gone! Isn't it? Disappeared.'

'Keep your hair on, Blonde-girl! Ha, get it? Keep your hair . . . oh, never mind.' G-Mamma finished poking around under the bed and sat up, flushed but triumphant. 'It's not gone. It had fallen off on to the carpet next to your box of goodies. We'll have to stick it harder next time. Here it is.'

Janey peered at the hair, which lay across G-Mamma's palm like overcooked pasta; shiny, limp and mushroom brown. 'Oh. OK. I think I was getting a   bit ahead of myself.' She giggled. 'Get it? A "head" of myself?'

'Hey, I do the jokes,' said G-Mamma sternly, 'and the raps. You just do your spying, like a good little Spylet.'

Janey smiled as she reached out a dampened finger to take the hair from G-Mamma. Pulling it closer to her face, she stopped abruptly. 'Hang on, G-Mamma,. This hair is darker than mine. Only a shade or two, but definitely darker.'

G-Mamma peered at it. 'I think it's just dirt, honey-child. Maybe you didn't vac under the bed quite as well as you should have done.'

'Oh.' It made sense to Janey. Twice now, they'd wet the hair with saliva, and hair certainly did get darker when it was wet. In between times, it had fallen into the dust engrained into the carpet. Of course it was dirt. Janey gave herself a mental shake, checked that nothing in the box had been disturbed and slammed the lid home, laying the hair carefully across the join.

'Can I go now?' said G-Mamma, waving the espadrille directions that Janey had brought upstairs. 'I want to run a few tests on this. And I've got croissants in the oven.'

'Sure,' said Janey. 'I'm going out with Mum now anyway.'

'Goody!' G-Mamma's voice got fainter as the metal panel at the Spylab end of the tunnel closed. 'I'd like an egg as big as my head, filled with Quality Street, please. Oh yay, a rap!

'An egg, choccy egg, as big as my head, With Quality Street, so good to eat.'

G-Mamma rapped on around the lab, probably dancing. It sounded fun. Janey would have liked to join in, instead of trailing around after her mum buying Easter eggs, but she scampered down the stairs anyway.

Sure enough, her mother was walking down the hallway, holding out Janey's denim jacket. 'It's still a bit chilly,' said Jean. 'Put this on, and I'll go and get the car warmed up.'

Janey thought enviously of Abe. Somewhere south. Somewhere warm! She looked at her pale reflection in the hall mirror and wondered what it would be like to get a tan. Maybe her hair would lighten in the sun. She might look more like Jane Blonde, all of the time! Her mirror image stared back at her, grey eyes fixed on her own as Janey reached up to touch the sore spot where G-Mamma had yanked out her hair. Thankfully, thought Janey, peering more closely at her reflection, her SPI:KE had only taken a couple of hairs, so she didn't have a bald patch or anything. She grinned. Sometimes G-Mamma was quite barmy.

Janey was still thinking this as she turned to the door, smiling to herself, when a chill rattled down her spine. She turned quickly back to the mirror. Her reflection gazed back at her earnestly. Janey smiled again, and the reflection smiled back. Wiggling her eyebrows, she was relieved to see Janey-in-the-mirror wiggle hers too. She must have been dreaming, but for a moment she could have sworn that when she was smiling at the mirror, the image in the smooth silvery surface had . . . had not smiled back. Even though her logic told her that it couldn't be true, Janey's spy nerve endings jangled ominously, and she quickly breathed all over the mirror as G-Mamma had just shown her. No marks. But if anyone messed with the mirror while she was out, she should be able to spot it when she got back.

Janey jumped into the passenger seat. 'Can I borrow your mobile, Mum?' She wasn't allowed her own, which was very funny when she thought about how many advanced gadgets she had in the Spylab next door. Jean handed it over as she drove off.

'Alfie!' said Janey into the mobile. 'Can you come over later? I've . . . I'm getting you an Easter egg.'

'Well, you don't have to bribe me,' drawled her friend. 'Mum's got me polishing the SPI-buys, and I'd have done anything to get out of it. But since you're offering, I'll have a chocolate orange.'

'All right,' she said. 'Come round after lunch.'

She followed her mum into the shop. 'Alfie's coming over afterwards. Hi mum wants him out from under her feet.'

'Oh, OK.' One mention of Mrs Halliday was enough to persuade Jean Brown. She thought the headmistress was marvellous, little knowing that she had once been her colleague, super-SPI Halo. 'Which one would you like?'

Janey thought about it for a moment, then walked over to the chiller section and pulled out a white carton of free-range eggs. 'I'd like these you know, like we used to do when I was little? I've got some glitter and glue and stuff. We could hard-boil them and decorate them tomorrow.'

Jean Brown hugged her daughter to her. 'You're a very unusual girl, Janey Brown.'

You have no idea, thought Janey as she squeezed back.

An hour or so later, they pulled up at home. Alfie was just riding up the path on his bicycle, which looked ordinary enough but which Janey knew to be a SPI- cycle, capable of going at immense speeds and even up the sides of buildings. He jumped off neatly, smiling at Mrs Brown. 'Just in time,' he said.

'You and your mother are so punctual, Alfie,' said Jean Brown. 'Must be a result of being such a good headmistress.'

Or being a super-SPI, thought Janey as she and Alfie trooped into the house after her mother. 'I'm going to give Alfie his egg now,' she said to her mum.

'Well, I'm going to have a nice bath and read the paper,' said Jean, heading off up the stairs. Once Janey was sure the door was closed, she beckoned Alfie over to the mirror.

'Couple of weird things,' she hissed. 'I put a hair over my SPI-buys box and it was like someone had moved it, although I did find it again, but it seemed . . . different. And then I was looking in this mirror and I'd swear . . . I'd swear my reflection didn't do what I did.'

Alfie's eyebrows shot up. 'What did you do?'

'I smiled like this.' She grinned at Alfie, and he took a step backwards.

'Weird. Don't think I'd smile back either.' Janey batted him on the arm. 'Be serious!'

Janey huffed all over the mirror, watching all the time as her reflection huffed back. There were no signs at all that the mirror might have been tampered with, but she blew again just to be sure. Suddenly Alfie appeared in the reflection too.

'Don't want to spoil your little steam-train impressions or anything,' he said, tapping on the mirror, 'but I think you've missed something. If there really was something weird about the reflection, then it must be something at the *back* of the mirror. Did you check to see if it's a two-way one? There might be someone on the other side!'

Janey smacked herself on the head. 'Of course! I forgot. You put your finger-nail against the surface, and if there's a gap between your nail and the nail in the reflection, it's a two-way mirror.'

'Like that,' said Alfie, nodding towards his fingernail, which didn't meet its reflection. 'What's behind here then?'

The two Spylets leaned forward, each reaching out a hand to take the mirror down from the wall and discover what was behind it. Just as they seized the edge, Janey looked at herself in the shining surface. Her grey eyes gazed back at her, perplexed, then suddenly turned away.

Janey's reflection spun sideways like a soldier on parade, so that Janey, very curiously, was suddenly looking straight on at her own profile. Then, in the next instant, Janey's mirror image disappeared out of sight.

Chapter 3 Double trouble

A rgh!' The mirror slipped through Janey's fingers and fell back against the wall.

'OK. Now I believe you,' said Alfie. 'Quick! This must back on to the ground floor of G-Mamma's house.' He wrenched the mirror off the wall; sure enough, behind it was a smoky window through which G-Mamma's downstairs toilet could be seen, squat as a burping bullfrog.

'Put that back or Mum will find it,' squeaked Janey. 'And come on!'

They took off through the front door and along the path to G-Mamma's house, peeking in at the windows as they ran. The ground floor of the house was a mystery to Janey. She had only ever seen the first floor which was entirely taken up by Spylab, and the back of the house leading to the garden. Of course, it should have occurred to her that G-Mamma must have some normal rooms like a bedroom, bathroom and proper kitchen – definitely a kitchen, given how much G-Mamma loved to eat.

Alfie shoved at the front door, but it was firmly locked and didn't so much as shudder under his fist. 'Thought so. G-Mamma normally must keep this locked when she's up in the Spylab so she can't be taken by surprise. There must be another way in.'

'Ring the doorbell!'

Alfie shook his head. 'She's got Puff Doodly on at a million decibels. She'll never hear us. Let's go the fireplace way.'

'We can't; Mum's upstairs.' Janey looked around. 'Round the back?' 'There's no way through.' Alfie kicked furiously at the wild overgrowth blocking the side path that would have taken them to the back garden.

But Janey had spotted something. 'Wait there.'

In seconds, she had bolted back to her own front door and leaped on to the seat of Alfie's SPI-cycle. She whizzed down her garden path and out on to the street, then turned in again at G-Mamma's gate, giving herself enough distance to get a decent run-up. Seeing what she was doing, Alfie threw himself on to the back of the bike. 'It's broad daylight. Are you insane?' he shouted. 'OK, don't answer that!'

'It's the only way. My reflection could be up to anything in there. We have to catch it, or at least warn G-Mamma. Hold on!' And Janey kicked off with her left foot, stood up on the pedals, and pounded the pedals around as fast as her legs could possibly go. The path was only short – in two seconds flat they had reached the front of the house.

'Wheelie – now!' screamed Alfie.

With all the strength she could summon, Janey hauled the bike up so that it teetered on its back wheel. It lurched towards the wall, and Alfie grabbed on tightly to Janey's waist as the back of his head plunged perilously close to the garden path. In less than a second, however, they were whipping up the side of G- Mamma's house like mercury up a thermometer. Next second: up the slant of the roof. Now past the chimney and down the other side. Janey held on, fingers rigid with terror, as the bike quivered for a moment on the edge of the roof and the ground loomed below them as if they were bungee jumpers.

But still she kept pedalling. One more second, and they were zooming down the bricks at the back of the house, just about taking in G-Mamma's startled eyes through the blinds at the Spylab window, and then they were off across the garden, skidding past the azaleas and avoiding the apple tree only because Alfie stuck his foot down and swerved them around it.

Janey took her feet off the pedals and they slowed to a clumsy halt just short of a bed of thistles. 'We managed to avoid that, at least!' she said thankfully, jumping off the SPI-cycle and looking around for signs of the intruder. There was not much to see, but over near the fence leading into the allotments that straddled the gully between her street and the next, she spotted two faint muddy footprints.

Alfie looked closely at them. 'They're really faint. Like they were only wearing socks or something.'

He's right, thought Janey. There was no tread imprinted into the flower bed, just the faint outline of a pair of feet. The only information they could possibly glean from this print was that the person had quite small feet and was wearing something with very smooth soles. 'Fleet-feet!' said Janey suddenly. 'That would explain why the two prints are side by side – they activated the foot jump to get over the fence.'

'The feet are around the same size as yours,' Alfie mused.

As Janey matched her foot-size to the prints, a window opened behind them. 'Spylets!' snorted G-Mamma, hardly able to contain her fury enough to keep her voice down to a whisper. 'Keep the noise down, hide that SPI-cycle, and get your bike-alicious booties back up here!'

'I think you're in trouble,' hissed Alfie as they made their way to the back door, opened by remote from the Spylab, and climbed the spiral staircase.

'Fancied a little joyride, did you?' said G-Mamma, pursing her orange lips until her whole mouth puckered like an aged tangerine. 'Just after lunch on a public holiday. Now do we think that was a a) a bad idea? Or b) a really really bad idea?'

From Alfie's sheepish expression, Janey could see that she was going to get no help. 'We had to, G- Mamma! We were looking in the hall mirror and my reflection turned around and walked off. Why've you got a two-way mirror in your downstairs loo? Anyway, we tried to find my reflection but it had disappeared . . . and so we had to SPI-cycle over the house to try to catch it!'

G-Mamma looked from one Spylet to the other, her Mermaid-Magic dazzled eyes twinkling doubtfully. 'Your reflection *ran off*?'

'I know it sounds weird,' said Alfie finally. 'Like Peter Pan and his shadow. But I saw it too, and there's evidence of spy activity. Two-way mirrors, Fleet-feet prints, hairs going missing . . .'

G-Mamma held up a hand. 'OK, no need for elaborate excuses, Spylets! Like I told Janey ten minutes ago, if you haven't got me an Easter egg, you just have to say.'

'But I haven't seen you for two hours,' said Janey. 'What do you mean, ten minutes ago?'

G-Mamma picked something up from the counter. It was a small woolly hat, bobbly and badly knitted, and nowhere near big enough to fit over G-Mamma's mass of curls. 'This little tea cosy. It was very lovely of you to knit it for me and all, Blonde-girl, but you should have known it's really not me styleee.'

'You can't knit, can you, Brown?' said Alfie.

'You're telling me,' agreed G-Mamma, poking a tapered silver nail through one of several holes in the hat.

'No, he means I've never even learned to knit,' said Janey. 'And I wasn't in here ten minutes ago. I've been out with Mum or downstairs with Alfie the whole time, since I saw you in my bedroom this morning.'

G-Mamma frowned, then pointed a remote control at the plasma screen dominating one end of the Spylab. 'Then who, Zany Janey and Alfie, um, Ralfie, is this?' Janey

24

stared at the screen, as Alfie seethed quietly about the "Alfie Ralfie" thing. The screen blinked and fizzed as some video footage burst into life – film from a security camera on the front of G-Mamma's Spylab fridge, judging by the angle from which it was taken: G-Mamma, moon-like and fleshy, extracting something from the fridge; G-Mamma at the computer, scanning the note from Abe; G-Mamma looking up in surprise as Janey walked in from the top of the spiral staircase, smiling awkwardly, wearing short khaki dungarees and a green tee-shirt, holding out the ragged scrap of knitting . . .

'That -that's not me.' Janey stared again as G-Mamma wound back the tape and the Janey-like figure appeared again in the Spylab, earlier in the day this time. On the film, a slightly blurry Trouble trotted over and rubbed himself around the legs of the imposter. 'I swear, G-Mamma, that is not me. I know it looks like me, but it really isn't.'

But if it wasn't her, who was it? Janey saw G-Mamma's eyes narrow as they went through the options. Judging by the Fleet-feet, it might be one Spylet disguised as another, which could be dangerous. Or, thought Janey breathlessly, maybe her father had once again Crystal-Clarified himself, and this time he'd come back as Janey herself. 'G-Mamma, do you think it's—'

'. . . time young Halo was going? Yes, I do.' G-Mamma shot Janey a warning glance across the room. 'Halo, tell your mother that something's afoot. I'm going

25

to give Janey a USSR. She might want to do the same for you.'

Alfie nodded, aware that something unsaid had passed between his friend and her SPI:KE, but too polite and well trained to comment. 'Right. I'll just rescue my SPI-cycle from the holly bush, and I'll get back straight away. Call me later, Janey?'

Janey nodded briefly. Her stomach was still churning from the sight of herself on the plasma screen, and the thought that it might be her dad. As soon as Alfie had left, she spun round to face G-Mamma. 'What if my dad's Crystal-Clarified himself again?'

'I don't think so,' said G-Mamma. 'If the other Janey was your father, he would have told one of us by now.'

Janey thought about it. That was probably true. Last time her father had reappeared as someone else, he'd tried to keep it a secret, but because of that Janey had thought he was an enemy until it was almost too late. 'OK . . . so who do you think the other me is?'

'I don't know.' G-Mamma spun the fridge around and fiddled with one of the pipes at the back. 'If you didn't have cast-iron alibis I'd have said that you'd been brain-wiped and it actually was you, but you didn't know what you were doing. That would be highly dangerous, Zany Janey. Whoever brain-wipes you could send you after any of our SPI secrets. Alternatively, you might have a doppelganger – a double, considered to be very bad luck. An omen of death, in fact. Some enemy might have found

26

your double somewhere and employed her to infiltrate Solomon's Polificational Investigations. If that's the case, they won't risk having two of you around for too long. Your life could be in danger, Blonde. I've got a *baaaad* feeling. Here, take this.'

She'd removed a small segment of pipe from the back of the fridge. It was solid, closed off at either end with a tiny combination lock. G-Mamma spun the minuscule dial with her eyebrow tweezers, and one of the ends popped open. With a flourish, she tipped the contents of the little safe on to Janey's palm, and Janey gasped as she recognized it. It was a diamond ring, very similar to the one Abe had given her mother a few weeks earlier.

'It's a spy ring!' she cried, slipping it on to the middle finger of her left hand.

'Yes, a USSR – Undetectable Spy-Shield Raiser. You spin the diamond, and an electromagnetic force field will spring up around you like an invisible tent. Very expensive, very experimental, and very very shiny.' G-Mamma was practically salivating as she looked at Janey's hand. 'You got spy-bling, Blondette! Use it carefully – like, for instance, when you go off to bed tonight. We need to make sure nobody's messing with your brain.'

'I'd better get going right now,' said Janey. 'Mum will be wondering what's happened to me and Alfie.'

G-Mamma nodded, a worried expression furrowing her brow as Janey left the lab. But it turned out that Jean Brown was not wondering about Janey at all. In fact, she was enjoying the fact that she could read the entire paper from front to back, including all the small ads, while her daughter sat in the armchair opposite her, reading quietly . . .

. . . just as Janey saw a few minutes later, when she opened the lounge door to find herself already there, looking right back at her with her own grey eyes.

Chapter 4 Twice as nice

Fortunately the door swung back against the sofa where Janey's mum was sitting, and Jean didn't see the two versions of her daughter, one calm and quiet in the armchair, and the other dribbling with disbelief in the doorway.

Naturally though, Mrs Brown was intrigued about who might have opened the door when both she and Janey were sitting there, in the same room. As she heard her mum lever herself off the sofa, Janey threw herself back up the stairs and hovered in the shadows on the landing.

'Must have been a draught,' she heard her mother say. 'I'd better start thinking about supper soon,' she went on. 'I think I'll make lasagne.'

'Mmmmmm, yummmm!' squeaked another voice. Now she was absolutely certain that the other Janey was an imposter – nothing Jean Brown cooked herself was ever going to be "yummmm'.

There was the strong possibility that Jean was in danger, so Janey prepared to creep downstairs, lure the other Janey out of the lounge without subjecting her mother to a sudden bout of double vision and take on the imposter. As she trod on the top step, however, the lounge door closed. Peeking down the stairs, she saw her double put a finger to her lips to stop Janey from calling out and then tiptoe up the stairs towards her.

Janey opened her bedroom door and allowed the doppelganger to walk straight by her. Coming into such close proximity gave her goose bumps and, reminded of what G-Mamma had said about bad omens, she flipped over the diamond in her ring and felt the slightest of tingles journey down her body as the force field enveloped her from head to foot.

Janey's double plonked herself on the bed, looking up at Janey with rather wide, scared eyes. 'Hello,' she said tentatively.

'Never mind "hello"!' Janey was pacing the room, too worried and upset to bother with niceties. 'Who are you, why do you look exactly like me, and what are you doing here?'

Biting her lower lip, the girl looked awkwardly at her feet. Janey was shocked to notice that there were tears in her eyes. Since she'd started using Ultra-gogs, Janey herself hardly ever felt the sudden need to cry that she often used to experience. 'I'm sorry,' said the girl. 'I just wanted a bit of alone time with her. She's so special, isn't she? I just sat and watched her read the newspaper. It was amazing!'

Janey sat down abruptly at her desk. This was seriously weird. The girl sounded pretty wimpy, and she'd found it fascinating watching her mother read? 'You've been watching me too, haven't you, and checking in with G-Mamma? What's going on? And don't try anything funny – I only need to smack the wall above the fireplace and G-Mamma and Trouble will be in here like a shot.'

'No, I won't try anything funny. I'm sorry if I've scared you, hanging around a bit secretively like that,' said the girl, looking anxious. 'I just wanted a bit of time to get used to you. It's been a bit of surprise to me, finding out all about you.'

Janey's eyes sharpened. 'Finding out what about me exactly?'

'Well,' started the girl, trying to gather her thoughts, 'it's difficult to know how to say this. Dad had a bit of trouble telling me too. And you're so much more . . . forceful than I am. Why don't I just say what he said? Yes. That's what I'll do.' She took a deep breath, and pinched the top of her nose, just as Janey used to do to get control of her emotions. '"Chloe," my dad said, just yesterday, "it's about time you found out about the rest of your family. You've grown up just with me. You've never known your mother, and you've always imagined she's dead."'

Janey stopped herself. She had been about to say that she had never known her father and imagined him dead until she found out the truth and became a spy. She looked closely at Chloe and saw understanding in her eyes.

'That's right, Janey,' she said. 'Just like you, only the opposite way round. You see, this family was split into halves. On one side, there was me and Dad. And on the other side was you – you and . . . and Mum.'

31

Janey's breathing grew shallow. 'What are you saying? What do you mean?'

'Sorry, how do I say this? Well, I'm your twin, Janey,' said Chloe.

Janey grabbed on to the edge of the desk. This was madness. She didn't have a twin – what was this strange mirror image talking about? 'That's not right. I can't have. Mum couldn't have had two babies without realising . . .' She felt sick, and she was shaking her head back and forth like a dog with a toy.

'I know it sounds unbelievable, Janey.' Chloe got up from the bed and came over to the desk, taking Janey's hands into her own identical ones. 'I had trouble believing it at first. But you know it's possible. Our father made himself disappear to save his family, but on the night we were born, he brain-wiped Mum — and took me away to live with him on the other side of the world. He left you here for Mum to bring up, so she never realised that she had been a super-SPI, or that she actually had two babies: you and me.' She squeezed Janey's fingers gently. 'You found Dad a while ago, and now you've got me too. A sister!'

Janey stared into Chloe's glassy grey eyes and felt her own welling up in sympathy. This was too much! It couldn't be right, could it? Although, as Chloe had said, she hadn't known anything about her past and her family until G-Mamma had turned up to begin her spy education just before her father had reappeared. At the thought of her father, a fierce gripe of jealousy soured her insides.

'So you . . . you've grown up with my . . . with Dad? Where?'

Chloe gave a little smile. 'New Zealand mainly, on some remote farms. It was pretty lonely. He wasn't around all that much, as you can imagine. You know what he's like for going undercover! But now he's planning on leaving the spy world, setting up a business and getting his family back together. He got in touch with you, didn't he? We've just moved to the first home we've ever lived in openly, on a sheep farm in Australia.'

'Australia!' Of course. Not just south. Really far south – right down in the southern hemisphere. That's what her dad had been trying to tell her in the espadrille "directions'. Which must mean that the espadrilles were a gadget, a gadget that would take her to him. She looked at Chloe. 'You don't have an accent.'

'Oh, sorry.' Chloe frowned. 'You see, mostly I grew up around Dad. He doesn't have one, so I don't.'

'But he must have been away a lot on his missions . . .'

Chloe's clammy hands slipped out of Janey's hands. 'Yeah, and I had a lot of nannies. I thought he was away lecturing or something. You know what Dad's like, Janey. Loves us so much, but needs to keep up with his spy work too. And look what he's done to do it! Told you he's dead, told me my mum's dead, pretended to be someone else . . .'

Janey knew Chloe was right. Her father *had* made her believe that he was dead. He *had* brain-wiped her mum. He'd invented a whole new persona for himself in the guise of his own brother, Solomon Brown. It all sounded impossible, which was why it made absolute sense that he would have separated his daughters for safety. Perhaps . . . perhaps it really *was* true. Chloe looked almost exactly like her, and she knew all their family background. Janey had a twin! A twin who had grown up with her beloved father. She couldn't help but feel envious, but then she supposed that Chloe was equally green-eyed about her growing up with their mother.

Suddenly she thought of something. 'When did you find out about Dad being . . . you know?'

'Only when he gave it all up,' said Chloe with a sigh. 'I'm quite sad really. I cry about it often. I'll never get to be a Spylet myself. Not like you, Janey.'

That explained why Chloe was so much quieter than Janey, more like Janey herself had been not too long ago, before she was exposed to a few death- defying missions, a mad SPI:Kid Educator with a rapping fixation, and a bunch of friends and family who knew all about the spying world. She couldn't help feeling sorry for Chloe. Maybe it was time to introduce her properly – as her . . . Janey could hardly bring herself to think it might be true . . . as her sister.

'Come on,' she said with a sudden smile, jumping up and prodding the wall above her fireplace at the ten-past-two position. With her hands behind her back so that Chloe couldn't see, she spun the diamond in the USSR to remove the protective force field. She wouldn't be needing it now. 'Let's go and tell G- Mamma.'

In the Spylab, Janey announced her arrival to G-Mamma by shouting, 'Ta da!' then helped Chloe to her feet. G-Mamma's mouth dropped so far open that a half-chewed raspberry-ripple chocolate fell out on to the worktop. 'Oh my life, it's double trouble!' she said hoarsely. 'Janey, what's . . . which of you is Janey? Holy Twinoly! if I stood you on the mantelpiece you'd be like bookends. What's going on?'

Janey grinned, pulling her sister forward. 'I'm Janey. There's not much to tell us apart, is there. Chloe's hair might be a couple of shades darker, but that's about it.'

'And Chloe is . . .?' said G-Mamma, fumbling behind her for her pearl-encrusted Ultra-gogs.

'My, err, twin.'

Chloe nodded, shrugged, chewed her lip and smiled all at the same time, as G-Mamma's eyes bulged. 'Well, for sure, that look is pure Down and Brown. But your twin? How?'

Janey repeated everything that Chloe had told her while her sister patted Trouble's head and gazed at G-Mamma with solemn, slightly watery grey eyes. G-Mamma listened intently, looking like a parrot on a perch, with her head on one side and her Ultra-gogs balanced on the end of her nose.

'Well, that is some story,' she said eventually. 'I'm going to have to come up with a cracker of a rap to cover that one. And meanwhile, young Chloe, you'd better stay with me until we hear more from your father about how he proposes to set up this little family reunion. Can't imagine how he plans to tell Jean she had two babies, not one.'

Janey looked at Chloe. 'That's true! Mum will go into complete shock! We can't both go down for supper in a couple of minutes as if it's perfectly normal!'

'No! I'm sorry! I didn't think.' Her sister looked very perplexed and suddenly slightly green. Her pale skin was damp, and strands of mousy brown hair stuck to her head. 'Is it supper already?' she said faintly. 'It's dark so much earlier here. I feel . . . I think I'm going to be sick.'

With that, she sprinted for the top of the spiral staircase that just peeked above the floor of the Spylab, making her way to G-Mamma's toilet with her hand clapped over her mouth and lank hair trailing behind her. Janey watched helplessly for a moment. Chloe probably wanted some privacy. When she hadn't reappeared in a few minutes, however, Janey took off after her, with G-Mamma and Trouble streaming behind her like the tail of a kite.

'Chloe!' she shouted as she powered down the stairs. 'Are you OK? Ow!'

As she reached the bottom step, Janey's foot made contact with a small slick of something slimy and slippery; she skidded straight off the staircase and landed in a heap in the downstairs hallway, with G- Mamma and Trouble just managing to stop themselves from falling right on top of her.

'My ankle!' groaned Janey. 'Yuck! She didn't make it to the bathroom in time – I just slipped in sick. Gross!'

G-Mamma squatted down to peer at the offending substance. 'It's very clear for sick. And it smells funny too.'

'Sick always smells funny.'

'No, sick smells disgusting, and this doesn't.'

Janey struggled painfully to her feet. 'Never mind the vomit analysis; let's check on Chloe! Can you help me? I can't walk properly.'

With Janey leaning heavily on G-Mamma, they staggered into the bathroom, but Chloe wasn't there. 'Kitchen,' Janey said and hobbled across to a room boasting another huge American-style fridge and no fewer than three microwave ovens, but no Chloe. G- Mamma parked Janey at a worktop covered in empty pizza boxes and trotted around the ground floor, opening doors and calling out Chloe's name.

'I think you might as well get in the Wower and cure that ankle-with-a-rankle,' she said, returning to Janey's side a few moments later. 'Your sister's skedaddled.'

It certainly appeared to be the case. There was   no sign of Chloe apart from the small pool of goo on the bottom of the spiral staircase. Janey sighed. This   is what life was like for spies – full of surprises, new meetings and sudden departures.

'Where, do you think?'

G-Mamma shrugged. 'Darned if I know, Blondey-Blonde. Maybe she fell down the toilet. She is a teensy leetle bit of a drippette.'

'G-Mamma, that's not nice. That's my . . . my sister you're talking about.' And she's just like I used to be, thought Janey with a wince.

'I know, I know. And boy, I'd like to SPI:KE that skinny twinny.'

Janey frowned. Her sister would never be SPI: KED, as she was never going to be allowed to be a Spylet. And that was all the more reason why Jane Blonde had to stick up for her. Somehow she had to find Chloe.

Chapter 5 Spinny twinny

Next morning, Janey was at the kitchen table, daubing paint and glitter glue on a hard-boiled egg. Her mum sat opposite, tongue out in concentration as she etched a beautiful daisy on to her own egg with fine silver leaf.

'Do one on the other side, Mum. Like twins,' suggested Janey. She peeked slyly under her lashes to see if there was any kind of reaction.

'Oh, I think that would be too much, don't you?' said her mother, painting in a fine green stem. 'Less is more, that's what I say. Twins would be such a handful. Look at Uncle James with Edie and Fen – two of everything, all the time.'

They were interrupted by a knock at the door; her mother came back into the kitchen with another parcel from her father, and this time it was addressed to Jean too.

'Easter eggs!' said Jean, holding her purple-foiled egg up to the sunlight. 'Isn't that sweet of Abe? I might have a little bit after breakfast.'

'Not me,' said Janey. 'I'm saving mine until Easter Sunday.' While her gold-wrapped Tweedledum and Tweedledee egg looked perfectly normal, she thought that she should probably open it in secret, just in case her father had tried to send her a coded message. It might even be the last spy message she would ever get, if Chloe was right.

ere was something else in the package – a small black boomerang about the size of Janey's elbow– but by far the most interesting item was underneath the eggs. Jean Brown held up a newspaper cutting, and Janey's eyes were immediately drawn to the large picture and article in the bottom-left corner of the front page. 'It's Abe!'

Jean Brown nodded. 'He's obviously in Australia. Looks like he might be getting quite wealthy too.' She squashed down a small sigh as Janey read the article:

A local sheep-farmer from Dubbo has the world of wool all of a dither with his new strain of merino sheep. They have straight hair that is more than a match in softness and usage for angora, and much easier to mass-produce. Says new farmer Abraham Brannigan of sheep farm Dubbo Seven: 'I've a background in genetics, so I've just bred the best strain of merino together with the lesser-known Andalusian mountain sheep, and this is the result – a super-soft, super-long-haired sheep.' Experts are claiming it's so good it could almost be knitted straight off the sheep's back.

Abe stood tall and handsome in the photograph, surrounded by his strange flock of long-haired, flat- eyed sheep. He was shading his eyes from the sun and grinning his film-star grin right into the camera. It was just as Chloe had said. Her dad was living on an Australian sheep farm, about as far away as possible, and causing a stir in the sheep world. Ice lollies, car washes and now sheep. There didn't seem to be any connection, but her dad did always seem to make a success of his business ventures.

Janey felt a little sad – firstly for her mum, who was finding it hard not to keep looking at the photo, and secondly for herself. Australia was a very long way away. A journey there by Satispy – spy satellite travel via space – would probably kill her, or at least leave her missing a few vital body parts. How on earth had Chloe managed to get her? And where the heck was she?

'Well, I'm pleased he's in business again,' said Jean suddenly. 'It's certainly done me the world of good, using some of his savvy.'

Janey stared at the picture. Why had he sent this, unless . . . 'Directions!' she barked suddenly. More directions. She just needed to find out where this farm was. And . . . find a way to get there.

As soon as they had finished painting eggs, she crept upstairs and sneaked through to the Spylab, holding the Easter egg and the boomerang from Abe.

'Another one. For me?' cried G-Mamma, grabbing the chocolate package as soon as it appeared through her fireplace.

'No, for me,' said Janey. 'It's from my dad. I thought we should take it apart very carefully and—'

'. . . eat it! Yes!'

'Nooo, analyse it carefully.'

'Oh, OK,' said G-Mamma sulkily.

They dissected the packaging as if they were carrying out a forensic investigation, with tweezers and little plastic bags for any evidence, and talcum powder for fingerprints. Running the prints on the box through G-Mamma's proved that it had indeed come from Janey's father, while the cardboard packaging revealed nothing out of the ordinary. The chocolate in the egg proved to be of very good quality, but definitely just chocolate. Only when they had pulled it apart into a series of tiny chocolate hexagons, one of which had somehow slipped between G-Mamma's teeth, did Janey notice that there was a letter on the back of each one.

'Look! Eighteen letters and a number 4. Nineteen, if you count the one you just ate, which I think was an O,' said Janey. 'It's like a giant anagram. Just give me a minute or two.'

G-Mamma wiped her mouth guiltily as Janey placed all the letters in a giant circle. She often found this was the best way to work out anagrams 'I'm guessing it's four words from the number. I think I've got the first one. B-E-W-A-R-E. Beware. This looks like . . . on . . . this. On this. Which leaves K-I-N-G-R- O-W. King row? Not the Sun King again, surely? Oh no! I get it. It's not that at all. It's W-O-R-K-I-N-G.'

'So what does the whole message say?' said G-Mamma, eyeing the letter W greedily.

Janey thought for a moment, and rearranged the words. 'I can't be sure, but I think it says: "Beware. Working on this".'

'Working on what?'

'I don't know.' Janey looked around. 'Something to do with chocolate? He's made ice lollies before. Maybe he's moving on to different food. Or maybe . . .' Suddenly she smacked her fist down on the counter. 'Of course! He didn't send a Tweedledum and Tweedledee egg for nothing! What are they?'

'Eggheads? Weird? *Alice in Wonderland* characters? Maybe Trouble's really the Cheshire Cat!' G-Mamma popped the letter K into her mouth. 'Don't worry, your father would approve. I'm just doing what every good spy does and eating the evidence. Yumptious.'

Janey watched her for a moment, then selected a few letters for herself. 'They're *twins*,' she mumbled through a mouthful of chocolate. 'Mum reminded me today that there are already twins in the family – my cousins Edie and Fen. He's warning me to be careful as he works on getting me and Chloe – and Mum, I suppose – back together again.'

'Twins do run in families,' agreed G-Mamma, peeling off her false eyelashes. 'Just dust this box off again,' she said, casting baby powder all over it. 'Yep. Abe again. Well, I think you should go and investigate your own twinette, in Australia. Down under cover. Ha! Get it?'

Janey swallowed hard. 'G-Mamma, I don't think the Satispy is ready for that kind of journey yet. I'd end up in bits.'

'There must be some way. Let's try that boomerang.'

43

Holding the boomerang aloft, G-Mamma peered at it this way and that, then drew back her arm and flung it across the lab. It spun around in a wide arc with a curious *choop-choop* sound, until it landed back in G-Mamma's hand. 'Really is a boomerang,' she said.

'I think it's those sandal things,' said Janey. 'He said "Directions" in the package, and now he's sent me some idea of where to go.'

G-Mamma studied the footwear curiously. 'They remind me of a prototype I tried ages ago, only they were boots with long laces that looked like Doc Martens.'

'Mum says these are called "espadrilles" or something.'

'That's it!' cried G-Mamma. 'ESPIdrills – that was the name. Earthmover SPI Drills!' She placed them resolutely at Janey's feet. 'I've not seen this type in action before, but your father obviously intends you to use them, so go and Wow, and take them with you.'

Janey dashed into the spy-shower cubicle.

G-Mamma was foraging around in a cupboard under the computer bench, but Janey could still hear her voice through the misty particles that transformed her from Chloe-lookalike Janey Brown to Sensational Spylet, Jane Blonde. 'I doubt that very much. Oh. You'll need this too.'

Janey stepped out of the Wower, self-consciously patting her high, sleek blonde ponytail into place as she saw what G-Mamma was holding. 'What is that? Some ancient diver's helmet?'

'It's not ancient at all,' said G-Mamma. 'Cutting edge, in fact. And when you get those eSPIdrills working, you're going to be very happy you put this on. It's SPIFFIG – that's SPI Furnace/Fire/Incinerator Gear to you. Go on. Helmet on, sandals at the ready.' Mystified, Janey followed G-Mamma down the spiral staircase and out to the back garden, putting the enormous helmet over her ultra-gogs as she went. As she wedged it down against her shoulders, a curtain of fine fabric fell down around her body, leaving only the eSPIdrills exposed.

'Now,' said G-Mamma, standing Janey firmly in an empty flower bed, 'if I remember correctly, you leave the ties open and spread out around you towards the compass points, like . . . so.' She trailed the leg straps of the sandals across the damp earth. 'And then we find a switch – ah yes, here we go, this funny little flower which isn't a flower at all, press in coordinates for Dubbo Seven – and we wait for you to get going.'

'Get going where?' whispered Janey, suddenly rather nervous. It felt as though little engines were revving up beneath the soles of her feet.

But before G-Mamma could speak, Janey started to rotate. Quickly.

'Spin to your twin, Janey baby!' crowed G- Mamma, breakdancing on the spot with delighted little claps each time Janey faced her again. 'Spin to your twin!'

Chapter 6 Earthmover

And spin Jane Blonde did. As she whipped round and around with ever-increasing speed, Janey found that she was sinking down into the flower bed. Daffodils and clods of earth flew in all directions, spat out by the long ribbons of her eSPIdrills as they spun like helicopter rotors, churning up the earth and forcing Janey down into it.

She was spinning so fast that the whole garden was just a blur of colour, and G-Mamma's face no more than a smudge of white and blue. Now she was on a level with G-Mamma's fluorescent pink wellington boots which appeared like an occasional fuchsia blip on a radar screen, and then there was nothing, only soil swirling around her. The feeling of nausea that had overcome Janey to begin with had gone, replaced by a light-headedness that prevented her from thinking straight. She wished she'd had some ballet training so she knew how dancers did dozens of pirouettes on the spot without either falling over or throwing up, but there'd been no time for any of that. Now she just had to allow her gadgets to do the work for which they were intended, and try not to think too much about it.

Further and further into the Earth she drilled, cocooned in a tunnel of soft brown dirt, then wet dank earth . . . harder clay . . . rocks, solid rock. Janey glanced upward as far as the SPIFFIG would allow her head to move; through the squashed worms and insects splattered on the clear dome of the helmet, she could just make out a tiny disc of starlit sky, no bigger than a pinprick. The top of the tunnel. G-Mamma's garden. Now she was buried many thousands of metres under the earth, with no clear idea when or where she would stop and how she would get out.

The SPIFFIG shifted slightly as Janey bore on through the layers of rock and took occasional plunges through water. The layer of material dangling from the helmet edge closed in around her and she shot through the Earth like a shrink-wrapped jelly baby, arms held rigidly at her sides and head enclosed in an enormous glass bubble. The SPIFFIG certainly stopped her from getting wet or dirty, while the eSPIdrills covered her up to the ankles so that her feet were protected too.

'Why was G-Mamma talking about fire?' Janey wondered after a few moments. Her silver SPIsuit would have done a good enough job, and if she'd needed more water protection, she could have put on a wetsuit.

But just as this thought bounced into her head, Janey noticed her feet warming up, and suddenly the dark earth strata she was whipping through were interspersed with layers of liquid red. Her feet and calves were now exceedingly hot, and the trickles of red were getting wider and more frequent, joining together until Janey was plunging through gleaming scarlet molten rock.

'Aaarghh!' screamed Janey. 'It's lava. Like in a volcano! G-Mamma, help me!'

But G-Mamma couldn't help, and neither could anybody else. Janey was trapped, searing her way through the ground, throwing up earth, rock, molten rock, then some kind of melted metal. Janey realised that the SPIFFIG was not only protecting her from intense heat; it was also withstanding monstrous pressure, millions of times what the body normally had to deal with. Janey would have been crushed into powder were it not for the brilliance of her SPI- buys.

'What now?' moaned Janey.

The eSPIdrills emitted a low hum, as though they were changing gear, and suddenly Janey wished she could put her hands up to her ears to take away the horrific shriek of metal drilling through solid iron. She must be at the centre of the Earth. And it sounded like the scariest ever trip to the dentist. Barely daring to open her eyes, she chanced a peek at her surroundings. There wasn't much she could make out through the grime on her SPIFFIG, but all around her was an amethyst glow, deepening here and there to a lustrous pewter grey. Metal. Glowing, solid metal. Janey closed her eyes and tried to think of Easter songs to sing as, rotating at a steady pace, the eSPIdrills sliced their way through the Earth's core.

Then in one horrible, terrible moment, the straps stopped turning and Janey came to an abrupt halt. Her breath came out in a great spurt, misting the SPIFFIG's dome. So that was it. She was buried at the centre of the Earth. Soon to be dead, in an iron coffin from which she could never be lifted. It wasn't the first time Janey had faced death, but it was probably the most hideous. Panic rose through her chest, making her gag, wishing she could claw at her throat, scream for help. But somewhere in her foggy brain, something clicked. Jane Blonde had to get to her twin and her father. She wasn't going to just wait for death to creep up on her. So Janey stamped her soles against the rigid iron of the Earth's centre and held her breath.

'Hallelujah!' she cried as suddenly, with a small jolt, the ties started to whip around again, and she resumed her thousands-of-revolutions-per-minute spin. She was on her way to see her dad. And her sister. And now it seemed as though she was speeding through the Earth, feet first, shooting through the rest of the iron core then the molten metal, and the lava, the rock, sand, water, more sand, until eventually she was whooshing through layers of soil and tree roots and insect life, and finally, with a slight smacking sensation against her feet, she broke through into the atmosphere.

Unfortunately Janey was upside down, with the top half of her body still buried in the ground, so she couldn't see who it was that grabbed hold of her feet and hauled her out of the earth. Hastily she dragged her hands across the side of the earth cylinder from which she was about to pop and pulled some scratchy grass as far as she could across

49

the hole; it wouldn't hide the tunnel completely, but it might stop anyone from discovering just how deep it was. To the untrained eye, it would appear to be just a shallow hole. Then, with a bone-crunching yank, Janey landed on her bottom on the warm ground and looked, dazed, at the tall figure looming over her.

'You digging for gold?' said a rough voice. 'Don't think you'll find any in these parts, mate. Best go and get your breakfast.'

'Breakfast? But it's . . .' Janey stopped short. She'd been about to say that it was night-time, but when she looked around she could see that it was anything but dark. She was sitting in a field, surrounded by sheep, with glorious sunshine glancing off her SPIFFIG helmet so that the stocky man had to shield his eyes. 'I know, I know,' he said, grabbing Janey's arm and hauling her to her feet. 'It's the holidays and you just want to play. But this is a farm. Don't make a nuisance of yourself, Chloe, love. Just an hour, and then you can play rabbits or whatever it was you were doing.'

Janey couldn't stop a huge smile breaking out all over her face. 'I made it!' She took the helmet off and popped it under her arm so that the man could see   her Jane Blonde ponytail. 'I'm not Chloe. I'm . . . I'm Janey, her twin.'

'Right, and I'm a day old,' said the man, giving Janey a gentle cuff around the ears. 'Go on, your dad'll be waiting for you.'

50

'No, it's true! I've just come here by . . . by helicopter, to see Chloe and Abe, who's obviously my dad as well. Look, my hair's a different colour and everything.'

The man cocked his head to one side.

'Look, I'll only be able to prove it to you when you see Chloe and me side by side. I know we're very alike, but there really are two of us.'

'All right,' said the man with a sigh, taking off his leather hat and wiping his forehead with a vast striped handkerchief. 'Let's take you to your father, if you're going to insist on playing your silly games. I've five hundred sheep to sort out, and frankly I don't have time to deal with you as well. Now move it.'

Janey walked alongside the man, trying to match his long, vigorous strides. The sun blazed down on them and there was no shade to speak of. After a moment or two of staring longingly at the man's hat, Janey put her SPIFFIG back on again. It might look peculiar, but after all, it was intended to keep out the heat, and it certainly did the trick quickly. Within a minute, Janey was feeling much cooler and could look around her through the glass filter of the helmet to take in her surroundings. Hanging back so that her new companion wouldn't see what she was up to, Janey fed her SPIV – her SPI Visualator – up past the lip of the SPIFFIG and held it close to her face.

'G-Mamma, are you there?'

G-Mamma's upside-down face appeared in the small screen on the SPI Visualator. 'Hello! Or should I say, "G'day"?'

'Yes, I made it,' giggled Janey. 'Right through the middle of the Earth and out the other side. This man is taking me to see my dad – he thought I was Chloe.'

'Right, give me a visual,' said G-Mamma. 'I'll check him out.' Janey turned the SPIV on her guide, who was striding out in front of her. 'Okey-dokey. Not sure how much I can tell from his back view, but you can update me later. What else can you see?'

Janey scanned her surroundings quickly. 'I landed in a field of sheep like the ones in that photo. There are hundreds and hundreds of them, and there are some other fields too. I think I can see some sheds and barns – might be where they do the shearing or something. We're walking towards a house, a wooden bungalow. It's really big. Hang on, we're just going past the barn nearest the house.'

Janey checked that the man wasn't looking and skipped off to one side. 'X-ray,' she muttered to her Ultra-gogs. It only took one glance, right through the huge barn doors, to recognize the glittering white furniture. This Spylab was the biggest she'd ever seen, with gleaming benches and large wheeled cabinets all around the edges of the great shed, and a huge space in the middle into which Janey's whole house – and G- Mamma's – could have slotted. 'It's a Spylab,' she said excitedly into her SPIV. 'Oh, and there . . .'

She stopped, shielding her eyes from the glare of the sun. It hadn't been that long since she'd seen the person standing on the veranda of the house, but still she felt joy fill her from the feet up. 'There's Abe. My dad's right there. Over and out, G-Mamma.'

Barely hearing G-Mamma's response, Janey dropped her SPIV and ran over to the two men standing on the wooden veranda. 'Here she is,' the stocky man was saying. 'Doing her astronaut impersonations.'

'Dad, it's . . .' started Janey. 'It's me.' She removed her SPIFFIG with a smile. '*Janey.*' And with that, she threw herself at her father. 'Thanks for getting me here.'

Abe grabbed Janey's shoulders and looked at her, his brown eyes filling with confusion, then hope, then sudden joy. 'Janey, you're here! You made it! How did you . . .? Oh . . . tell me later. You're here, in one piece, and what a sight you are. Bert,' said Janey's father, turning her round to face the other man, 'this is my other daughter. Chloe's twin.'

Bert's kind, leathery face crumpled with disbelief. 'Strewth,' he said. 'You weren't telling porkies then? Sorry, Janey. You and Chloe just look so alike!'

'Identical twins.' Abe put an arm around Janey's shoulder and hugged him to her. 'Peas in a pod. They were . . . well, it's a long story. Some other time perhaps. Right now, we ought to reunite these sisters and prepare

53

the place for Janey to stay – for a long time, I hope. Hungry, Janey? Let's get you some breakfast.'

They walked around the veranda to the back of the house. The aroma of frying bacon licked the air. From within, Janey could hear fat spitting and pans being scraped. In a moment, Janey would see Chloe again. Chloe, with her father. Their father. Janey's very own Abe. Suddenly she wished she could have him to herself for just a little while longer.

'It's great to see you, Dad,' she said softly, putting her hand on his arm.

Abe patted it gently, turning to her with a smile and a small shake of the head as if in wonderment   that he could have both of his daughters in the same place at the same time. 'You too, Janey. Better than you could ever imagine.'

He dropped a kiss, clammy from the rapidly rising temperature, on to her forehead, and with her arm tucked inside the crook of his elbow, Janey walked into his home.

Chapter 7 Dubbo seven

'J aney!' Chloe waved a spatula at her from the vast country range. Huge heaps of bacon, tomatoes, mushroom were already mounded up on four plates, and Chloe was just adding eggs to the ensemble. 'Sorry, I hope you don't mind . . . I heard your voice, so I got another plate out.'

'You made all this yourself? It looks delicious!' Janey was highly impressed – the most she could do herself was zip things through the microwave.

Bert helped himself to one of the plates and sat down at the scrubbed kitchen table. 'Have to be able to cook on a farm, Janey. There aren't too many shops or takeaways nearby, so you have to do things for yourself. This bacon was running round the field last week.' He shovelled two rashers into his mouth and beamed cheerily. 'Oink oink.'

Suddenly Janey wished they were just having toast. It must have shown on her face, as her father laughed loudly. 'He's teasing you, Janey. Grab a plate and eat up.'

Reluctantly Janey took her portion of food from Chloe. 'The bacon's not really bacon, it's turkey strips,' whispered her sister as she slid a fried egg on to Janey's plate. 'Don't tell Bert I'm trying to cook more healthily! He loves his food.'

'Like G-Mamma,' said Janey. She smiled at Chloe, who was pink-cheeked and glowing from the heat of the stove – she certainly looked a great deal better than the pale, sweat-slicked person who had run off   to be sick. 'We were looking for you the other night.'

Chloe's face fell. 'Oh, I'm sorry. It was rude of me to just disappear like that, but I was . . . embarrassed   at getting ill, and I didn't really want anyone seeing me that way. I hope you understand?'

'I do.' Janey understood perfectly. She too used to spend a lot of time feeling humiliated. It seemed her sister had not progressed quite as far as she herself had done. Like Janey had used to be, Chloe often seemed on the verge of tears, and she was nowhere near as sure of herself as Janey was since she had become Jane. She looked at her father to find him staring from one to the other of them, eyes glittering with awe and a strange hint of . . . what was it? Janey couldn't quite put her finger on it.

She sat down next to him. 'Thanks for sending the stuff and the picture and everything. It made it so easy to get here and find you.'

At Janey's words, the room grew very quiet. Abe gave a slight shake of his head, Chloe stared down at the table with her lower lip caught between her teeth, and even Bert stopped chewing for a moment. Gauging the mood in the room, Janey reached a quick understanding of the situation: Bert didn't know about her father being a spy. He wasn't another G-Mamma or a Halo. He was a sheep farmer, pure and simple.

Abe changed the subject quickly. 'What would you like to see, Janey? More of the farm?'

'I could show you my room!' Chloe jumped up excitedly, looking at Abe for agreement.

'Sounds great.' Janey pulled at her SPIsuit self-consciously. 'Although I'd like to get changed first. It's a bit hot in this! Can I de-W . . . have a shower?'

Abe shook his head quickly. 'Sorry, Janey, there's a bit of a drought round here, and we have to save as much water as we can for the sheep. Plus, it's solar heated so it's much better in the evening. Maybe later you can have your one shower for the day. But I'm sure Chloe could lend you some clothes. You take Janey now, Chloe, and I'll meet you at the sheep pen in a few moments.'

Janey followed her sister, watching enviously as Bert and her father donned their leather hats and strode away. Now that she'd met up with him again, she was very reluctant to let Abe out of her sight for any longer than she had to. But as a consolation prize, she decided as she took in the polished wooden floor and the stamped tin ceiling painted a peaceful buttery yellow, having a new sister to get to know was pretty exciting.

Chloe threw open her door and ushered Janey into her room. It was many times the size of Janey's bedroom but with slightly less furniture, so that the big wooden bed, the rich oaken chest of drawers and the enormous kidney-shaped dressing table sat on the polished floor like islets in a gleaming brown ocean. Through the window, the view was of sparsely grassed fields and the odd eucalyptus tree for as far as Janey could see.

'Here you go – do you think these will fit?' said Chloe, pulling clothes from the chest.

'Well, I expect so, since we're exactly the same size!' said Janey with a grin.

'Oh, of course. Sorry.' Blushing, Chloe turned her back politely as Janey removed her SPIsuit and pulled on some jeans and a cotton shirt. This was a first – still Jane Blonde, but in ordinary clothes. Once Janey had shaken out her ponytail, the twins looked even more alike, with only the tinge of gold in Janey's hair making it clear which of them was which. 'You'll need a hat,' said Chloe, passing Janey a black baseball cap and putting on an identical one herself.

Janey laughed. 'Poor Bert will never be able to tell us apart now! What's this?' She pointed to the emblem stitched in gold on to the cap – a large number seven with the word "Dubbo" arched over the top like a crown.

'Oh, sorry. I should have explained. It's the logo Dad designed,' said Chloe. 'Dubbo Seven: Dubbo's the nearest big place, and seven's because we've got seven hundred acres. At least, that's what Bert thinks – Dad made him change it to make it spy-like, although Bert hasn't even got it!'

The lettering reminded her of something, but Janey couldn't quite bring it to mind as she followed Chloe out through the big front door. Far in the distance she could see two small figures leaning on a fence. 'Come on,' said Chloe. 'We'll go on the four-by-four or it will take us forever.'

To Janey's delight, they clambered atop a chunky four-wheeled motorcycle and whirred off across the paddocks. It reminded her a little of the go-kart Alfie had created from a suitcase when she'd first met her dad, and with a sudden pang she remembered how far she was from her friends and her home. Alfie would love it here, she thought. Her mum too, sitting at home longing for sunshine, would be overjoyed to be here surrounded by her family.

With a gentle skid, the quadbike puttered to a stop and Chloe and Janey wandered over to their father and Bert. From their stiff bodies and flushed faces, Janey guessed they were having an argument.

'They need the vet, mate! You can't sell them with great bald patches on them,' Bert said huffily. 'My name would be ruined! And they'd just send them back anyway.'

Abe sighed. 'All right. Just put these in the far paddock, and I'll have a look into it. And don't bother with the vet; try to remember you're just the overseer around her now. *I'm* in control, so it's my name we need to worry about.'

As Abe turned around he rolled his eyes at the girls. Bert stomped off moodily, slapping a few of the sheep on the rump to get them moving beyond the fence and into the next field. Where they had been standing, clumps of silky beige wool littered the ground, and Abe walked behind Bert, picking them up and shoving the wool into a large plastic bag.

'Come on, girls, you can give me a hand,' he said, passing each of them a bin bag.

Janey tried not to notice that he had handed a bag to Chloe first, and she scurried around the paddock, unlooping the fine wool from the fences. 'So what's wrong with the sheep?' she asked.

'Nothing!' said Abe sharply. Janey looked up in surprise, but Abe was already looking apologetic and walking over to her. 'They're moulting for some reason, but it's nothing that I can't fix. It's complicated, Janey. You read the newspaper article about how I'd done it – crossing a merino with . . .'

'. . . an Andalusian mountain sheep,' finished Janey. 'Yes, it sounded very clever.'

Abe grinned. 'It's even more clever than that, actually. I haven't crossed the merino with another sheep at all, but I can't tell anyone that. You see, what I've actually created is a sheep – this prize- winning merino with fabulous form, sturdiness and wool production – merged with the creature from which we get angora. A rabbit.'

'A rabbit?' Janey stared at the prize-winning sheep, half-expecting it to start bouncing around the pen. It didn't look as though it would win any prizes now. It had lost more wool than any of the others, all from its back, so that its coat started halfway down its sides and straggled to the floor around a great bald patch, like some kind of mad monk. The woolly creature regarded her balefully, a sad and longing look in its eyes, so that Janey had to resist the urge to run over and give it a hug. 'It's half-sheep, half rabbit?'

Her father had previously turned frogs into mice, humans into ice sculptures, and people into other people, so this was definitely not beyond the realms of possibility. Abe shook his head, however. 'No, I just spliced the angora hair gene together with the sheep breed. One of my more brilliant moves, I think! I've now got these award-winning sheep that are going to make me a fortune, and we can live off that. I'll no longer need to be a spy.'

Ever since Chloe had mentioned that their dad was going to give up spying, Janey had been worrying. Being spies was in their make-up, in their genes, yet now, it seemed, all the spies she knew were no longer going to be able to fulfil their role in life. Because one thing was certain – if her father stopped being a spy, Solomon's Polifications Investigations would lose its heart, its rhythm. SPI would never be the same again. She sighed. 'Are you sure about that, Dad? Isn't it what you've always loved doing?'

There was a sudden gleam in his eye, but it disappeared just as quickly. 'I thought so, Janey. I've thought that for such a long time. But other things are more important. Family. Not getting killed. Having you and Chloe back together again, and being able to live with you like a normal father. That's what matters to me now. This way, out here in Australia among the sheep, it's all a possibility.'

Somehow, while Janey couldn't argue with that, she still felt saddened – uncomfortable even – about the family giving up spying. She handed Abe her bag of wool and walked over to close the gate behind the mad-looking sheep. There was a strange but familiar odour in the air, and Janey looked down to find herself her foot hovering over a small patch of vomit. Chloe vomit. It was exactly the same as the sticky little pool Chloe had left on the spiral staircase. She looked at her sister anxiously.

'Chloe, are you feeling OK?'

Chloe shoved a scrap of wool into her plastic bag. 'I'm fine. Why?'

'No reason,' said Janey quickly. She didn't want to point out a pool of sick to someone who didn't want to admit it.

'Oh that!' said Abe, bounding over to Janey's side. 'Chloe, I think Janey was wondering if you'd been sick. Don't worry, Janey; it's just sheep food. It's a special diet we have the sheep on to keep their genetic make- up stable. Out in this heat, it just melts.'

'So why don't you use some other food?'

'I'm working on it,' said Abe tersely. The heat was clearly getting to him as well as to the food.

'Right,' said Janey, taken aback. 'I'm . . . I'm sorry, Chloe. There was some on the stairs, and I thought you'd . . . you know.'

'I did feel ill, but I made it to the loo. Whatever you found must have been food on my shoes,' said Chloe with a small smile. 'It happens a lot. Sorry. I hope you weren't too worried about me? I really shouldn't have put you to all that trouble. I just needed to get home quickly – you know how it is – but it's no excuse really . . . I shouldn't have just disappeared. You and G-Mamma and lovely Trouble must have been really upset. I'm so sorry.'

She looked so abject that Janey couldn't help herself – she ran over to Chloe and gave her a hug, and her sister, after stiffening slightly, smiled and squeezed Janey too. 'It wasn't any trouble.' Janey meant it – it was no trouble at all, having family surrounding her.

The rest of the day passed quietly, with the relentless sunshine broken only by occasional stop-offs at the house to eat lunch and an afternoon tea of huge date scones made by Bert, piled with cream and jam. When they weren't eating, Janey and Chloe followed Abe around the farm, checking fences, picking up stray wool and bouncing over furrows in the quad- bike. It was all very pleasant, although Chloe was quiet and didn't really say much unless Janey asked her a question. Janey didn't mind; she was happy to soak up the sunshine and the closencss of her dad and her new sister.

Only when the sun began to swoop low behind the eucalyptus trees did she think of the time. 'Yikes, I've been here all day. What time is it at home?'

'About 5.30 in the morning, Easter Sunday,' said Abe, checking his watch.

Janey winced. 'Oh no. Mum will be up any moment. I'd better go.'

At this Abe and Chloe exchanged glances, and suddenly Abe laughed. 'Look at your sister's face, Janey. She's so disappointed! Look – stay. We can get a message home for you.'

Janey herself was reluctant to leave, but her mum had spent every Easter morning since Janey was big enough to crawl laying trails of Easter eggs around the house and garden. She'd be frantic if Janey wasn't there to do her egg hunt. She shook her head. 'No, I'd better go. But I'll come back soon.'

Abe looked at her with his head on one side, and then nodded. 'Make sure you do. We'll miss you. Now why don't you go back with Chloe and put your SPIsuit on? I've got some things to do in the Spylab, but I'll come and say goodbye when you're ready to go.'

Janey and her twin quad-biked their way back to the house and made their way to Chloe's room. As Janey got changed, Chloe sat down at the immense dressing table and started brushing her mousy hair.

'You're so lucky getting to be a Spylet, Janey,' she said sadly. 'I so want to be like you. Would you . . . Could

I brush your hair for you before you go and   I have to go to bed? I could put it back in your Jane Blonde ponytail for you . . . if you like.'

She said it in such a quiet, timid little voice that Janey's heart went out to her. It was much earlier than Janey would have had to go to bed, and she wondered, just for a moment, whether Abe was a stricter parent than her mum. He was sometimes a bit short with Chloe, she'd noticed. 'Sure,' she said, handing Chloe the brush. 'We'll have to be quick though.'

Actually she found it quite relaxing, and so, clearly, did Chloe. Before too long her twin had closed her eyes and they both settled into the calming rhythm of the brushstrokes. Janey's eyes were nearly closing too, made heavy by the hot, still air, the constant buzzing of the flies at the window, and the quiet shhoooosh . . . shhoooosh of the hairbrush . . .

Just as she was about to nod off, a fly buzzed in her ear and Janey snapped to attention. Chloe had stopped brushing and was dozing quietly, still just about upright, her lank hair sticking moistly to her scalp and a faint grey sheen tainting her skin.

'Chloe!' said Janey urgently, but her sister lolled back against the bed and gurgled softly in her sleep.

Janey put down the brush, which was suddenly slightly sticky and unpleasant to touch, then grabbed her SPIFFIG and scampered out of the house across to the

Spylab. 'Time at home!' she yelled to her Ultra- gogs. 5.50 a.m. blinked across the lenses. She had no time to waste.

Abe was bending over the tonsured sheep that Janey had noticed before, but turned quickly when he heard her footfall. 'Chlo– oh, Janey, it's you!'

Janey ignored the sheep's sorrowful eyes and pulled at her father's arm. 'I don't think Chloe's very well. You should go and see her. I've got to get home, but I'll be back as soon as I can.'

'No, Janey, stay. I—'

'Mum will be expecting me any minute. Oh, thanks for my Easter egg. Bye, Maddy!' That seemed an ideal name for her for the poor mad-monk sheep.

Janey threw her bemused father a kiss and sprinted off across the paddock. She cast occasional glances over her shoulder, and before too long she could see her dad carrying her sleeping sister over to the lab. He'd look after her there. Her Ultra-gogs gave her clear vision even in the fading light, and with her speed enhanced by her Fleet-feet she very soon found herself at the entrance to the tunnel through the Earth. Laying out the straps of her eSPIdrills, Janey made sure her SPIFFIG was on straight, pushed the small embroidered flower to "ON' and began the crazy journey back through the very centre of the planet.

And it was only when she was very nearly home, close to daylight and Easter-egg hunts, that she realised something that made her very sad: not once had Abe mentioned her mother. Janey would have to do something about that. And soon.

Chapter 8 Easter feaster

G-Mamma seemed incredibly excited about her Easter eggs. As soon as Janey appeared at the top of the spiral staircase in the Spylab her SPI:KE jumped to her feet. 'Happy Easter, Blonde!' she cried. 'Now, where's that egg?'

'G-Mamma, don't you think I've had more important things to do?'

'More important than supplying me with chocolate? I don't think so!' G-Mamma clapped her hands. 'I've got an egg rap for you. Here goes!'

'No . . .' began Janey, but her godmother was already swaying to the beat being pumped out by the computer, while synchronized patterns waved madly across the screen. G-Mamma pointed dramatically at Janey.

'Now don't you make me beg For my choc-a-late egg
Been waiting all this time For the choccy to be mine Milk, white or plain,
Yeah, to me it's all the same It's yummy-yummy-yummy
When it's in G-Mamma's tummy

And with that she shook her belly at Janey, then beamed and opened her arms expectantly. Janey laughed.

A mad-looking sheep was nothing next to G-Mamma. 'I'll have to go next door and get it for you in a minute. But first of all I'd better de—'

'De-code, de-brief, de-Wow, oh yeah!' chanted G-Mamma, walking like an Egyptian around her make-up bench. 'Phew! I am in the ZONE, Janey baby.'

Janey called out to G-Mamma over the Wower's hum as the glistening droplets and sleek robotic hands turned Janey from Blonde to Brown, while still filling her with enough effervescent energy to survive yet another day on no sleep at all. 'My dad's not going to be a spy any more – he wants to sell the wool from those sheep. And that man who you saw in the SPIV is Bert, who's helping him. Bert doesn't know a thing about spying. Oh, and Chloe's really good at cooking! But she can be a bit wimpy, and I feel a bit sorry for her really. Must be lonely out on Dubbo Seven with no friends around. I think Dad would like me there full-time, but the weird thing is –' she stepped out of the Wower cubicle in black jeans and a pony-print T-shirt – 'he never said anything about my mum. Maybe he's scared she won't be interested after he disappeared on her? Anyway, I can sort it out for them.'

'Whoa there, Missy Matchmaker.' G-Mamma held up a hand. 'One step at a time. I've been writing down a list of the things to check out for you – Dubbo Seven, Bert the sheep man, the rabbity wool, and I think we should look into the sick gunk. Not that I'm concerned about anything, but I wouldn't be doing my job if I didn't double-check these things . . .'

'I didn't bring any. Oh! Wait a minute.' Janey looked around for the eSPIdrills. Trouble was sniffing at them suspiciously, no doubt puzzled by the strange new aroma emanating from the sandals. 'Yes! I stopped near the gate to get some wool; there was some of the gunky stuff there, so now it's on my shoe. There, under those bits of wool.'

G-Mamma scraped some up with the end of her little fingernail. 'I'll analyse it. You better go and see mummy dearest – and get my egg . . .'

Janey rolled her eyes at G-Mamma and smiled as she slid on her ASPIC through the tunnel to her room. She could hardly believe that it was Easter Sunday, after having already spent all of the same day in Dubbo. She felt like a time traveller. Hearing movement on the other side of her bedroom door, Janey jumped to her feet, whacked the tunnel activator to close the panel and stepped out on to the landing.

'There you are!' said her mum, hugging her tightly. 'I thought you were never going to get up. It wasn't so long ago that you used to wake me up at five thirty for your egg hunt.'

'Crikey, did I? You must have had to lay the trail really early!'

'Or the night before. Many a time in my dressing gown and wellies, stumbling around in the dark. I must have looked like the loony next door.'

Janey gave her mother a kiss. 'Is it ready now?' 'Yes, but it's a little different this year . . .'

Janey followed her, puzzled. Normally she headed to the kitchen, and the trail would take her round the garden, up and down a few trees then back to the lounge where her "big" egg would be waiting. This time, the first egg – one of the ones they'd boiled and painted together – was lying on the top stair. The next was two stairs below, with another two steps below that. She stepped carefully, picking up eggs as she went, until she reached the bottom of the staircase with five eggs balanced precariously across her interlinked hands. She was quite relieved that they were hard- boiled. The sixth and final egg had been painted by her mum; it was lying on the hall floor, a large purple arrow outlined in gold glitter, pointing to the lounge. Janey pushed open the lounge door carefully. There on the coffee table was an enormous box of Ferrero Rocher and a stack of banknotes.

Her mother paused in the doorway behind her. 'I've been thinking, Janey. You're not a tiny girl any more. Soon you'll be going to a different school and growing up, and maybe going off to college or university one day, and it's my job to make that easy for you. So this is a special kind of egg. It's called a nest egg.'

'What's a nest egg?' said Janey, picking up the wad of cash. 'I thought you were saving up to go on holiday.'

'Never mind that.' Jean smiled at her. 'We can set you up with a bank account, and you can add to it whenever you get any birthday money or whatever, and then if you ever need it, you'll have some money behind you.' She looked at her daughter anxiously.

Janey grinned, and gave her mum a gigantic hug. It was typical of Jean Brown to think how she could protect her daughter as far into the future as possible. And in his own way, her dad was doing the same, by not allowing himself or his family to get into dangerous situations. The sooner they could all be together again, the better.

'It's a fantastic egg,' she said firmly. 'And now *I'm* going to do some eggs – fried, with bacon.' If Chloe could do it, Janey decided, then she could do it too.

In the end she scrambled the eggs in the microwave, and her mum helped to grill the bacon, but it was still the first breakfast Janey had more or less cooked, and her mum looked at her proudly as they splashed brown sauce over their plates.

'Happy Easter, Mum,' said Janey. 'Happy Easter, darling.'

One day, Chloe and her parents and Janey would be able to sit down together somewhere and swap eggs and jokes and stories. With that in mind, Janey smiled secretively and ploughed through her breakfast.

Later, Jean dropped her off at the Hallidays and disappeared to see how Abe 'n' Jean's Clean Machines was faring. Easter Sunday should be busy at the car wash.

'Thanks,' said Alfie, relieving Janey of his Chocolate Orange as soon as she got inside the house on the school grounds that he and Mrs Halliday lived in. 'I've not had nearly enough chocolate today.'

Janey assumed he was being sarcastic, as he usually was. 'I'll have it back if you don't want it!'

'I'm serious! Janey's here, Mum,' yelled Alfie down the corridor into the kitchen. 'We're just going upstairs to eat some CHOCOLATE.'

Mrs Halliday appeared at the kitchen door with a tea towel in her hand and a dusting of cocoa across one cheek. 'Hello, Janey. Happy Easter. Now don't go acting all hard-done-by, Alfie Halliday. I'm still making a chocolate Easter cake, like I always do.

Perhaps you and Janey could manage a piece a bit later. Provided you don't eat too much beforehand of course,' she added darkly.

Janey grinned as she followed Alfie upstairs. 'What is it with these mums?' she whispered. 'It's hard to believe our parents are all superspies. Oh, sorry.'

It wasn't just their mothers who were superspies. Both their dads were too, only Janey's was a good spy while Alfie's was evil overlord Copernicus. He'd only found that out during the last mission, and as usual his face closed up at the mention of parents. It was very hard to accept that his dad was the enemy, frozen and out of harm's way in some secret location guarded by SPI agents, and Alfie clearly wasn't happy talking – or even thinking – about the whole thing.

She changed tack quickly. 'Your room's unusually tidy.' Janey was used to having to pick her way across a quagmire of quietly rotting football gear, half-built model aeroplanes, piles of books and the odd pizza box.

Alfie pulled a face. 'I know. Disgusting, isn't it? Everything put away and tidied up. Mum got a bit of a bee in her bonnet when I told her about your little visitor and insisted I clear everything away so I could tell if anyone's been in here.'

'And have they?'

'Only Mum!' Alfie rolled his eyes. 'She's become this demon cleaner. I've hardly got any clothes left to wear – as soon as they hit the floor, she scoops them up and puts them in the washing machine.' Cracking open his Chocolate Orange, he handed Janey a segment and chose a large chunk for himself. 'She's even started taking my handkerchiefs.'

Janey looked at him in surprise and suppressed a laugh. 'I thought only old men used handkerchiefs? What's wrong with tissues?'

'You obviously haven't seen what the Wower does to a tissue,' scoffed Alfie. He wrestled opened the top drawer of his bedside cabinet, which bulged with enough pristine white silk material to stuff a pillow. 'This is how they come out when you Wow them. They're all kind of slippy; honestly, you can't wipe your nose on them. It's revolting. Anyway, I think Mum must have got sick of it, because now she's taken to taking the tissues out of my pocket while I'm asleep.'

Just as Alfie was proving his point by attempting, with no success, to wipe his chocolatey fingers on the glossy surface, Mrs Halliday called upstairs. 'Alfie, Janey, I think you'd better come here.'

'Probably wants me to wash up,' said Alfie sulkily. He pointed at Janey. 'If that's it, you're drying, OK?'

'OK.' It was probably worth it for a slice of Mrs Halliday's chocolate cake.

But when they got downstairs, Alfie's mother was standing at the door under the stairs that led to their cellar Spylab. 'We've had a message from your father, Janey. He seems to have sent it to everyone in the SPI group. But I think we need you to decipher it, Janey.'

Janey raced down the steps and over to the computer, with Alfie and his mother close on her heels. The message, entitled "Happy Easter", had been sent from the Sol's Lol's headquarters in Scotland, so it seemed genuine – but wasn't her father in Australia?

'That's odd,' she said.

Janey double-clicked on the attachment and a little slide show began. The first image was a fluffy yellow chick, pecking at something invisible to begin with, then turning to face them directly and opening and closing its beak. The second was a list of zodiac signs, with Gemini, Libra and Aquarius highlighted. Next was a beaker and jug; the jug poured water into the beaker; once it got to the top, an arrow flashed on and off, pointing to the level of the water. Finally, a picture of a couple of steaming hot pies hanging from a long-curved meat hook popped up, and as they watched, the image of the pies faded into nothingness.

Janey clicked on the slide-show icon again and watched carefully as it progressed. 'It's a bit complicated. I need to write it down. I think the first word is BEAK. That's what the bird's showing us. I don't understand the second one, but the third one, I guess, means FULL. And then that last one . . . pies going?' She peered closely at the screen, and then wrote down her arm: BEAK ? FULL, and then a little picture of a pie.

'Let's have another look at that second slide,' said Mrs Halliday. 'They're zodiac signs, aren't they? I don't know much about them, but just hang on.' While Janey stared at her arm, Maisie Halliday typed "Gemini, Libra, Aquarius" into the Google bar and waited a moment. 'They're all air signs,' she said, reading from the screen. 'I've no idea what that means, but that's what they have in common.'

'Great.' Janey inked the word AIR between the two words on her arm, and then flicked back to the final picture. 'Ah! I've got it. I thought that was a sort of meat hook, but it's not.'

'What is it then?' said Alfie a little crossly. He was never as quick as Janey at working these things out. But then, she had been trained in code breaking.

76

'It's an S.' Janey scribed the letter S on to her arm, and thought about it for just a moment. Then she nodded. 'That's it. BEAK. AIR. FULL. S – Pies fading away.' Alfie and his mother looked at her expectantly. 'It's a warning. "Be careful. Spies disappearing".'

For a long moment the spy and the two Spylets looked at each other, almost as if they expected the others to fade away before their very eyes. Her father always warned them, somehow, when danger was imminent, but it looked as though they were all OK. She would have to get back to Dubbo Seven very soon though. Then Janey gasped. 'We're all right, but G- Mamma's on her own. I'd better get home.'

'I'll give you a lift,' said Mrs Halliday, veering off when she got to the hallway and reappearing with a large parcel in her hands. 'Take your mother some cake. I don't think we'll have time to eat it.'

'Mu-um,' moaned Alfie.

His mother poked him in the ribs. 'Never mind the cake, Spylet. There's danger about. Move!'

Chapter 9 Spylet spirals

Together they ran to the car and piled in, with only the slightest tussle for the driver's seat as Alfie realised it was still full daylight and he couldn't risk being seen at the wheel. They careered around corners until, just moments later, they pulled up outside Janey's house. Piling out of the car with Janey in the lead, the three of them headed straight up G-Mamma's path. Janey high-kicked the door down and they shot up the spiral staircase, pausing only briefly to jump across the gap that had appeared between the top of the spiralling steps and G-Mamma's Spylab floor. She glanced at it quickly and then bounded across the lab.

'What the magic gadget are you doing?' cried G-Mamma, leaping up so far that the top of her voluminous Easter bonnet nearly hit the ceiling.

'G-Mamma, you're here!' Janey ran over and grabbed her SPI:KE's hands in relief. 'There's an email from Dad.'

'Greetings Halo, Baby Halo.' G-Mamma waved at the Hallidays, ignoring Alfie's snarl. 'Yes, I saw the message. Didn't understand what the bejeepers he's talking about, of course.'

'It means, "Be careful, spies disappearing."' Janey turned to the computer and pointed to the slideshow. 'Ah,' said G-Mamma, trying to look mysterious. It was very difficult in her milk-maid's outfit. 'It might say that, but it also says it came from Scotland.'

'Yes, from Sol's Lols,' agreed Janey. 'I know Abe's in Australia, but I got there and back pretty quickly,' she went on. 'Maybe he's travelling to and from Australia by Satispy or something? Or perhaps he has his own eSPIdrills.'

'Those DMs,' said G-Mamma with a gleam in her eye. 'He's got them working properly.'

'Or maybe the message is fake,' said Alfie. 'Designed to make us all panic. Look what we did – legged it out of our house like it was going to explode. There could be evils all over it by now.'

'Alfie's right.' Mrs Halliday was looking very thoughtful. 'Janey, you should go to your father and find out why he sent this message. I'll tell your mother you're staying with us for a day or two when I take this cake round. Alfie, you go with Janey. Then G-Mamma and I can check things out around here.'

'But how?' Janey held up the eSPIdrills. 'I am NOT wearing those,' said Alfie.

'Well, you'll have to stay here then,' said his mother.

Janey, however, was thinking of what she had just had to do to get into the Spylab. 'Hang on. When Chloe left, she did it from the ground floor of G-Mamma's house. And I've just had to jump off the steps because the spiral staircase seems to have shifted . . .'

At this, G-Mamma and Maisie Halliday stared at each other. 'Swirling steps, they've finished the design,' said G-Mamma, sprinting over to the staircase.

'And you've got one here. Of course!' Mrs Halliday raised her hands. 'Naturally the first people to use it would be his own two children. Come on, Spylets. You can take the stairs.'

'We're going to climb down steps to Australia?' Alfie's eyes bulged.

'Are you sure it's ready?' said Mrs Halliday to G-Mamma. 'They hadn't had approval, as far as I'm aware.'

G-Mamma shrugged. 'Sol's had them installed, so I think they'll be OK. Janey, get in the Wower!'

Bewildered, Janey skittered across the Spylab to the spy shower cubicle and slammed the door behind her. A minute later, Jane Blonde emerged in her silver lycra, black Ultra-gogs and Girl-gauntlet. Clumsily, she pushed the USSR spy ring on to her left hand as Alfie went to Wow up into his denim-coloured SPIsuit, Boy-battler and slender metal Gogs.

G-Mamma raced across the floor, strapped on Janey's ASPIC with frantic speed, and then, to Janey's disgust, shoved a pea-sized object up her nose. 'Euw! G-Mamma!'

'It's a SPINAL cord,' said G-Mamma, tipping Janey's head back and ensuring the gadget was wedged properly in place. 'SPI Nostril-Activated Litmus. The string descends from your nose and analyses strange smells. I haven't got anywhere with the sick gunk, but this might do the trick.'

To Janey's relief, once she'd got used to the sensation of having something lodged in her nostril, it wasn't too uncomfortable. She and Alfie followed G- Mamma to the spiral staircase. 'This is amazing,' said the SPI:KE. 'SPI must have planned this all along!'

Alfie snorted. 'It's just a spiral staircase. They're not that unusual!'

'It's not just a spiral staircase,' said his mother sternly. 'It's cutting edge SPI technology. Still a bit experimental, I suppose, but no more so than the eSPIdrills. This, son, is indeed a SPIral staircase. A SPI Rotating Air-Lock staircase. You'd better get in.'

To the Spylets'' amazement, when G-Mamma said 'Unlock' in an authoritative voice, the metal steps began to move. Sliding outwards, each step pivoted so that it lay on its side, and then flipped down to form a raised join with the next step. After a few seconds they found themselves standing next to a large hollow tube, rounded off at the top and ridged all the way down its black metal sides like a centipede. The central pole on which the steps had been mounted now stood alone in the middle of the capsule, and when Janey peeked over the edge she could see it stretching down into the depths. 'Do we slide down it?' she asked. It looked like the longest fireman's pole she'd ever seen.

Alfie shook his head. 'No way. And anyway, it reminds me of something. It's like a . . . a lift shaft.'

'Stand back!' ordered G-Mamma.

The next moment the floor quivered beneath their feet, and they all tottered backwards as a vast blast of air exploded into G-Mamma's house, quickly followed by the smooth arrival of a lozenge-shaped capsule, black and gleaming as an earwig, that swivelled up to meet them, turning like a screw. A panel slid open, and Janey could see that they were being invited to step inside a rounded cubicle a little smaller than the Wower. 'It is a lift,' she said softly. 'An underground one, or rather – a through-the-ground one.'

'Hence the reason it's an airlock. Always a bonus to be able to breathe.' G-Mamma straightened Janey's Ultra-gogs and shoved her inside. 'There are straps top and bottom for your hands and feet. Make sure you don't grab the pole in the middle. It will probably get pretty hot.'

'I'll go and distract Jean,' said Mrs Halliday, holding aloft the bag of chocolate cake. 'Good luck, Halo. You too, Blonde.'

Alfie ducked inside the SPIral before his mother could give him a kiss in public, and Janey watched as he strapped himself in. 'We'll SPIV as soon as we get there,' she said to the G-Mamma, now standing there alone.

'Buckle up tight!' G-Mamma had the same feverish glint in her eye that she always had when trying out a new gadget. 'It may be a bumpy ride. Or it may not! Who knows?' And her beaming face beneath a ribbon- tied Easter bonnet disappeared from view as she proclaimed, "LOCK!" and the panel of metal between them drew shut.

Alfie looked around him. They were completely sealed into the metal tube, with only a sprinkling of star-like lights at either end for illumination. He pumped his Boy Battler and it lit up like a large round light bulb. 'I don't like this, Blonde. What's going to happen?'

'Well,' said Janey, 'if my eSPIdrills are anything to go by, we're going to start to spin, any minute.'

But when it started, it was nothing like the rapid rotating effect of her spy shoes. There was a slight hum, a long, dizzying moment of silence, and suddenly they were off, corkscrewing through the Earth in great looping rotations that made Janey's stomach lurch as if she was on a fairground ride. Alfie groaned and backed up against the wall, while Janey did what she could to hang on to the chocolate orange in her stomach. No wonder Chloe looked sick if this was the way she went to and from Australia! Janey felt as though her head was being pulled out through the soles of her feet.

'How long does this go on for?' Alfie looked green in the white light radiating from his Boy-battler. 'I need a bucket!'

'I don't know! It seems faster than the eSPIdrills, but somehow the pressure feels worse.'

There was nothing they could do now. There was no button to press to send them back to G-Mamma;   in fact, the only controls they knew were 'Lock' and 'Unlock' and they certainly didn't want the door springing open as they shot through rivers of boiling lava. The only consoling thought was that Chloe had been all right after she'd used it – if indeed, that was how she'd travelled, and G-Mamma hadn't got it all wrong . . .

The temperature was soaring. Their faces and left hands – the only parts not covered by protective spywear – dripped with sweat, but Janey had been through worse, and she was now getting used to the plummeting sensation. No wonder Chloe always looked slightly green and clammy – too much of this type of travel and Janey would look the same way. She dared to take in a deep breath, and instantly found herself cooling down.

'Breathe in, Alfie – the air close to us is not too bad. Keep away from the walls and the pole in the middle.'

Alfie shuffled his strapped feet away from the walls and gulped down some air. 'That's better. Yeah, it's . . . it's not too bad now. Hey, are we slowing down?'

Janey nodded as a hissing sound vibrated around them. 'We must be going through the water table. That's not that far from the Earth's surface. We're nearly there.'

In just a few moments the feeling of movement ceased. 'Unlock,' said Janey clearly, and they stepped out into the balmy Australian night.

Chapter 10 Down down under

They emerged from the SPIral staircase on to a platform high up in a wall of the Dubbo Seven Spylab.

'What's that?' whispered Alfie. Somewhere nearby they could hear retching sounds.

'Probably one of the sheep.' Janey held up her Girl-gauntlet and angled the laser light around them. Right at that moment, a sheep bleated plaintively from somewhere within the metal walls of the Spylab.

'No, *that* was a sheep. I think the puking thing was a stowaway.' Alfie stepped into the darkness, bent down and grabbed something. It yowled in a highly offended fashion. 'Yours, I believe?'

Trouble dangled forlornly from Alfie's Boy Battler, his whiskers and Spycat quiff drooping like week-old cut flowers. 'That'll teach you to sneak in where you're not invited,' said Janey in a stern voice, but Trouble looked so repentant and sick that she couldn't really be angry. 'Come here.' Nestled under her arm, Trouble soon started to purr.

'What time d'ye reckon it is?' said Alfie.

Janey shrugged. 'I'm not even sure what day it is any more. But judging by the sky, it must be nearly dawn. Let's go and see the sheep Dad and Chloe wake up.'

She walked over to the paddock, with Trouble lodged on her hip and Alfie hoovering down great gulps of air. It was quite cool without the blaze of the sun, and they found after a few moments that they could speed up and bounce along on their Fleet-feet. Janey passed the hole she had made with her eSPIdrills and stopped to drag a tumbled-down fence post across it; there was no way she wanted Trouble trying to get back to G-Mamma via that route. When she caught up with Alfie, he was staring into the empty paddock.

'Do you think your twin comes here to be sick whenever she's used that SPIral thing?' Alfie pointed to the little puddles vomity dotted around the field. 'I mean, I don't blame her, but it can't be very nice for the sheep. No wonder there aren't any here.'

'No, it's melted sheep food, apparently. Maybe the flock's been moved while it's cleaned up or something. There was that one we heard up at the Spylab.'

'We might as well go back there,' said Alfie. 'Wait for your dad to get up.'

It seemed to be the most sensible thing to do, so they headed back to the wooden bungalow. 'By the way,' said Janey, 'the sheep farmer, Bert, doesn't seem to know about us all being spies, so don't give anything away. G-Mamma's checking him out right now.'

'That must be him, is it?' Alfie pointed to the broad-shouldered figure standing on the veranda.

'Looks like him – it's too short to be Abe.'

Alfie stopped short. 'Hang on a minute. Abe is your dad? I thought he just worked for him?'

Janey could have kicked herself. There was no way of getting Alfie involved in this mission without him knowing a little bit about how Boz Brilliance Brown had transformed himself into Abe Rownigan, but since she had got into so much hot water last time by letting tiny bits of information slip out, it was critical that she didn't give everything away – not even to her best friend and fellow Spylet. She had to tell him *something*, and much as she hated lying to Alfie, she figured that half- truth would serve them both pretty well. He'd have to know that Abe was Sol/Boz, but not that the SPI leader had Crystal-Clarified himself into a complete new person.

'Yes, it's a disguise,' she said eventually. 'My dad made himself up with that clever plastic stuff they use in movies – latex, you know.'

'But Abe's about a foot taller than Boz!' Alfie raised one eyebrow, but then got distracted by Bert's penetrating stare. 'What's he looking at?'

Janey grinned and grabbed Alfie's arm, dragging him over to the veranda. 'Hello again, Bert. It's me, Janey.' She waggled her ponytail brightly. 'This is my friend Alfie. Dad knows him already.'

'Thought so,' said Bert slowly, looking Alfie up and down. 'Weren't you over at Abe's laboratory barn?'

Janey groaned inwardly. He must have seen Alfie as they left the barn a few moments earlier. She really didn't want Bert wondering why they'd been snooping around, and stumbling across SPIrals and SPI gear.

'Yes. No. Sort of,' said Alfie, not very convincingly. 'I was just trying to find Abe to say hello, but, you know, he wasn't there.'

Bert put on his hat. 'Must have gone to get a bit of shut-eye at last. He works all night in that lab of his, and then farms sheep all day. It's a wonder he can stay awake. Still, it's early yet; I think we can let him and young Chloe have a lie-in. Why don't you guys come with me while I catch up with the sheep?'

'They're not there,' said Alfie helpfully.

'That's what I mean about your dad, Janey. Spends all night in that lab *and* moves the sheep around. They're probably out the back of the barns. That's where he normally has them overnight.'

They wandered together past the shearing sheds and out past the barn housing the Spylab. 'Is that a cat you're holding?' Bert peeked under Janey's arm at Trouble. 'Looks more like a possum.'

'Oh, this is Trouble. He followed me from . . . from home.'

'G'day, Trouble,' said Bert amiably, chucking the cat under the chin. Trouble rubbed his fur against Bert's gnarled finger and purred ferociously. Bert smiled at Janey's surprised expression, and she noticed how his lined and grumpy face lit up instantly. 'They all love me, animals. Don't they, puss? Yeah. Now, where's me other little beauts?'

The sheep were indeed milling around in the large pen a field or so away from the Spylab. Janey pointed out Maddy to Alfie; the massive bald patch on her back made her easy to spot. The other sheep all looked pretty lustrous and well-groomed, ready to go to market, but it was the patchy Maddy who baahed merrily, kicked up her back legs, and scampered over to Bert. 'She's the nicest one, isn't she?' said Janey to Bert. 'Even if she looks a bit manky.'

'Always was my favourite, this one.' Bert made a fuss of the sheep, who had suddenly stopped and was eyeballing Trouble mistrustfully. 'She's the only original sheep from the days when it was just my little old sheep farm, before Abe bought me out and asked me to stay on. These other ones – I don't like them so much. Don't go telling Abe, will ya, but they're a bit boring. No personalities. They even all bleat the same.'

'Don't all sheep bleat the same?' said Alfie.

Bert looked at him, a little askance. 'I'm picking you don't know much about sheep, son. Of course they all say "baa" in a similar way, but if you listen you'll hear that they sing it out at all different notes in the musical scale, and some of them say "maaaa", and some say, "nerrr", and each one's unique. But not these sheep here. They look perfect and they sing in perfect harmony. Boring, like I said.'

'What's Maddy's bleat like?' asked Janey. 'Maddy?' Bert laughed. 'Her little call is specially for me. Paaaa.'

'Paaaa,' bellowed Maddy obligingly, and Janey and Bert burst out laughing.

Alfie curled his lip in disbelief. 'Talking sheep,' he muttered. 'As if.'

'You should have a bit of respect for your elders, son,' said Bert, 'and for the gifts that nature provides us with, and that includes sheep. Whether they talk or not.'

'I . . . I'm sorry.'

Janey pointed towards the house, glad of a diversion. 'There's Abe. Dad!'

Abe's approaching figure seemed to pause, then speed up dramatically. Her father arrived at a run and skidded to a halt before them. 'Alfie, I . . .' He stopped abruptly and peered closely at Janey's Spylet friend. 'It really is you! You came with Janey? I'm so glad to see you!' And he threw his arms around Alfie, much to the Spylet's surprise.

Janey was also a little shocked, especially as her father seemed barely to have registered her presence. 'We thought we'd come together,' she said, adding pointedly, 'Dad.'

Abe laughed and grabbed Janey for a hug. 'Well, I did see you only yesterday – just a few hours ago. I haven't seen Alfie in so long! How are you? How's your mother?'

'F -fine,' said Alfie, slightly overwhelmed.

'Great.' Abe beamed at everyone, then dropped a kiss on to the top of Janey's head. 'Tell you what, Janey: there's a bit of man's work to be done out here just at the moment. Why doesn't Alfie give us a hand, and you can go and wake up your sister? We can all have breakfast together soon.'

Janey's jaw sagged. So not only was she going to be upstaged by Chloe, but now Alfie too! And since when had her father been interested in what was 'man's work', when spying was all he'd done so far, and he thought she was good enough for that? For the first time, she felt really mad at her dad. He might be going straight so they could all be together again, but 'straight' didn't seem to equate to 'nice'. Even Trouble wasn't making his usual fuss of him.

'Right,' she said stiffly. She looked at Alfie, hoping he'd decide to come with her, but he simply shrugged and said, 'You're the boss! Let's go! See you later, Janey.'

Abe nodded with his film-star grin, and then shouted after her, 'Oh, Janey! Take the ugly one back with you, will you?'

The ugly one? Maddy the sheep looked around with what Janey could swear was hurt in her eyes, and Janey knew just how she felt.

'Come on, Maddy,' she said, tucking Trouble further under her arm. 'Let's go and find Chloe.'

Maybe then, at least, someone would be interested in seeing them.

Chapter 11 Love or hate

A fter a slow walk of constant reassurance and reintroductions, Trouble and Maddy were getting along famously. Trouble jumped down from Janey's arms and slithered around Maddy's legs in his normal sign of acceptance, and the sheep was positively skittish, kicking out her legs in an invitation to play. She might be ugly, thought Janey, but she was certainly full of pep. Eventually Maddy allowed Trouble to be placed on her back as she shouted 'paaaa' to the skies. Trouble sat on her bald spot like a badly fitting toupee, and they trotted along together quite happily as Janey checked in with her SPI:KE.

'G-Mamma, Blonde here,' she said into her SPIV, after first ensuring that nobody was around to hear her. The face of her SPI:KE appeared upside down.

'Go to it, Blondey.' Her head was popping from one side of the little screen to the other, more or less in time with a thunderous bassline that made the SPIV jump on Janey's chest.

'G-Mamma, what's that noise?'

'Oh! Sorry, forgot about that. Just, with your mother being away, I thought I'd pump it up. Oh yeah!'

'WHAT DO YOU MEAN, *MY MOTHER'S AWAY*?'

G-Mamma's face disappeared for a moment as she turned down the music. 'She's gone away. Must have decided on a little holiday for herself when Maisie told her you were staying at their place. I've checked the phone bug and she didn't make any bookings on there, but she probably did it online.'

'Without me? She's gone on holiday on her own?' Janey could hardly believe it. But when she thought about it, her mum could have said exactly the same thing when Janey suddenly disappeared. She sighed. 'I don't blame her really. Anyway, nothing new, apart from Dad seems to have gone all weird and macho. I haven't had a chance to ask him about the message yet. Have you found out anything new?'

'Yes. Bert Lester . . .' said G-Mamma, and Janey could see she was staring at the computer screen. 'Nothing on him other than what we know already: Abe Rownigan bought the farm from him a short while ago, just as Bert was about to go under, so he agreed to work for Abe as his sheep-farming expert. But Abe is clearly the real expert. You'll never guess what your dad's up to now, Janey!'

Janey paused, hardly daring to ask. 'What?'

'Well! Mr Genius Genetics has been at it again with his splicing. I got the full analysis on that wool. No wonder it's so fine . . .'

'We knew that already,' said Janey. 'It's made of merino wool spliced with angora rabbit fur.' 'There's no rabbit in there,' said G-Mamma

seriously. 'It's hair, Janey. Probably human.' 'But . . . but that's disgusting!'

G-Mamma crumpled face filled the whole of the SPIV. 'Pukesome! I got rid of that hat Chloe knitted pretty sharpish. But it's pretty clever, when you think about it. And he's disguised it really well. If this wasn't a Spylab, we'd never have found out.'

Janey looked down at poor Maddy. Her coat, or what was left after handfuls of it had fallen out, didn't look at all like hair. It was thick and greasy with lanolin, as Janey would have expected wool to be. But she wrinkled her nose as she thought of the other sheep with their long silky coats. 'That's vile. Look, I'm at the house now. I'll call in later.'

'Righty all-mighty. And by the way, I helped myself to my egg as you never gave it to me. And that cake Maisie had made – your mum hadn't touched it. I'm the Easter feaster!'

Is it *still* Easter? thought Janey as she let go of her SPIV. She really had no idea what day it was, and if breakfast hadn't been mentioned she wouldn't have been too clear what time it was either. But Chloe was in the kitchen, rather pale but moving steadfastly around the kitchen.

'Two more for breakfast, Chloe!' Janey smiled at her from the doorway.

Chloe spun around. 'Janey! That's nice. You brought your cat. Does he have a full breakfast too?'

'No, the other one's for Alfie.'

'Oh, sorry! What must you think? Full breakfast for a cat! I'm ridiculous sometimes. Ridiculous!' Chloe's shook her head as her eyes filled with tears.

Janey stared after her, perplexed. She had to help her sister toughen up, somehow. 'You're not ridiculous, Chloe.'

'But I'm not like you. Sorry Janey. I won't cry,' said Chloe, but her face remained pinched as she fed bread into the toaster and slopped water into the vast tea-pot.

Janey had no chance to say anything more as her father entered the room with Alfie. They both looked tired – the "man's work" must have been every bit as hard as her dad had suggested. 'Alfie, I know you've sort of seen her before, but . . . this is my twin sister, Chloe.'

'Hi,' said Alfie shortly. He sat down next to Abe and waited for Chloe to put his plate in front of him, then wolfed down his food as the family members ate theirs at a more leisurely pace. At least Abe had stopped firing questions at him, thought Janey, which was just as well as he was obviously too ravenous to talk. She forked her food down, wondering why the mood was so sombre. Bert had gone off to see a potential sheep- buyer for another breeding programme, and it was so quiet around the table that Janey quite missed him.

'Sorry we're not very chatty, Janey,' said her father after a while. 'We've got a big contract coming up, the biggest we've had – a couple of hundred sheep, all at once. It'll set us up for life.' And he winked at her so that she could see she was included in the plans for the rest of his life. Janey couldn't help but smile back, although she did wonder when he planned to mention her mother. He'd mentioned Alfie's after all.

Much, much later in the day, when all the sheep had been inspected and groomed and moved down to the lower paddock in which Janey had first seen them, Janey cornered Alfie. He'd been avoiding her all day, and she was more than a little hurt. 'Do you think my dad's acting a bit weird?'

Alfie shrugged. 'Nope.'

'He hasn't asked about my mum yet, even though he asked about yours.'

'So?'

'Well, he wants us all to be family together again, but that has to include my mum.'

'Sure. He's just waiting for the right time.'

'I suppose so,' said Janey. Alfie stared at the sheep he was grooming. 'Do you know what else? G-Mamma says that this wool is merino sheep mixed with . . . human hair.'

'Yeah, right,' said Alfie flatly.

It was hard going getting any response out of him. He really must be tired. 'I haven't seen Dad on his own yet. Did you ask about the email?'

'It's genuine, OK. He SPIraled to Scotland and sent the message just as a reminder for people to be cautious.'

'What? "Be careful, spies disappearing" is just a general warning?'

At this, Alfie threw down his brush. 'Not "disappearing", just "disappear". In general, spies have to be careful. That's all. Honestly, Janey, am I supposed to cross-examine people, like . . . all the time?'

'Um, yes.' Janey hadn't seen Alfie like this before. He could be pretty sarcastic, and regularly got into spats with his mum, but he never really got wound up like this. 'We're spies, remember?'

'Spylets. That's what we are.' Alfie shook his head angrily. '*Little* spies. Abe is a superSPY, and my boss, and I respect him. So I'm not going to snitch on him, to you or anyone else.'

'But I don't want you to sni– He's my *dad*, and I love him more than you do!' Before Janey knew what was happening, tears were flowing down her cheeks for the first time since she'd become a Spylet. She'd had a real row with her best friend, and got into a competition about who loved her dad more. She couldn't believe it! But of course *she* was the one to whom he meant the most – he might be Alfie's beloved boss, but he was her father. Family. Flesh and blood. Why was Alfie acting like this?

'You two,' said a deep voice suddenly, sounding out a warning note. Abe was leaning against the fence, watching them curiously. 'Not falling out there, are you?'

Alfie spoke first, concentrating hard on the back of the sheep before him. 'Course not. Janey's my best friend,' he said in a flat voice that didn't sound very convincing.

'Janey?' said Abe.

She looked at her father, unable to say anything, eyes misty with tears, and the beginnings of a runny nose which reminded her of the SPINAL cord she had stuffed up her nostril. Right at that moment she really wished for one of Alfie's stack of handkerchiefs.

'All right,' said her father. 'Time we wrapped up anyway. Why don't you go ahead let Chloe know we'll be in soon, Janey. Alfie can help me do these last few sheep. Use your Fleet-feet if you like – Bert's still out of town so you won't get seen by a non-spy.'

'But, Dad,' said Janey, trying to hold back the tears. 'I want to help. What did you mean by your message? Spies disappearing? Which spies?'

At this, Abe looked at Alfie, who shrugged. 'You told me earlier, remember? Spies always have to be careful, because they are known to disappear.'

Abe nodded slowly. 'That's it, Janey. Just as Alfie says. You should listen to him, you know.'

'Right,' said Janey, choked. She did listen to him. She always listened to him, when he was being her friend. But not when he was sucking up to her dad like this!

She dashed back to the house, using the speed of the Fleet-feet to pound out her anger on the parched grass. At the door, she stopped and called out for Chloe.

'In my room,' came the reply.

Chloe was at her dressing table, combing out her thin beige hair. She looked at Janey in the mirror. 'Oh dear. You look all hot and bothered.'

'I am a bit.'

'Well, good job you have a sister now.' Chloe stood up and gestured to Janey to sit in her seat. 'Let me brush your hair again. It's really relaxing.'

Janey felt a sudden rush of warmth for her twin. It *was* nice to have a girl to talk to and do girly things with, particularly if Alfie was going to start turning on her too. 'Thanks, Chloe.'

'No problem.' Chloe removed the silver band holding Janey's blonde ponytail in place and began to pull the wide brush through her hair in long fluid strokes. In no time at all the brush had established a calm, soothing rhythm. Brushhhh, pause, brushhhhh, pause, brushhhhh . . .

It was quite hypnotic. Why was I upset? thought Janey, yawning. Why did I cry? Jane Blonde doesn't cry. Janey Brown cries, but not Jane Blonde. Chloe cries too, but not Jane . . . She looked up at the mirror to see if her eyes were red, but the reflection swam in front of her. Chloe was looking rather sickly and wan again, but Janey blinked the image away. Jane Blonde never cries, she thought. It was a comforting thought. Never cries . . . She could just go to sleep . . . Jane Blonde go to sleep . . .

And just as she was about to nod off, she heard a tiny whisper, a familiar voice, Abe's voice, her *father's* voice, just creeping into a tiny space inside her head: 'Jane Blonde, I despise you. Despise you!' She felt a terrible pain in her legs as she fell to the floor.

Chapter 12 Clones and chloe

It was Trouble, leaping on to her lap and sinking his talons into her thighs, who brought Janey round from her dream-like state, although in reality the dream had been more like a nightmare. Janey gulped. If her father hated her, it would be unbearable. For a while she lay curled up on the floor, staring into the hypnotic green eyes of her cat as he nudged her gently with his plushy nose.

Something was wrong, she knew it. The voice couldn't have been a real voice but it was a symptom of something – some niggling doubt in her mind – that was making her very uncomfortable in the small kernel of emotions that sat inside her chest telling her what was right and what was wrong: her spy instincts. What was going on? Of course her father didn't hate her. But he was very distracted, and now her best friend was acting strangely, and her sister was sickening for something. Suddenly, at the thought of her twin, Janey jumped to her feet. What had happened to Chloe? One minute she'd been there brushing Janey's hair, and the next she was gone.

'Come on, Trouble,' said Janey. Together they ran through the house, checking the bathroom, the kitchen, even her father's spotlessly tidy bedroom and Bert's little suite of rooms at the back of the kitchen. There was nobody around. Checking that Trouble was still at her side, Janey ran out on to the veranda. Still nobody. Across the patch of land separating the house from the outbuildings, one small square of light was etched on to the grass. 'The Spylab! Of course.'

Janey sprinted across to the door of the laboratory, Trouble trailing in her wake. As they got closer to the door, however, their journey became much harder. A strong wind had whipped up out of nowhere; sandy earth, tufts of grass, and the odd knot of sheep's wool flew around Janey's head. She felt like Dorothy in *The Wizard of Oz*. 'Crikey, Trouble,' she gasped, leaning into the wind to try to reach the laboratory door. 'A hurricanes. We'd better warn everyone.'

Just as the angry gust of wind died away, she reached the barn door that led into the Spylab and leaned on the doorframe, catching her breath. She'd been wrong about the light. There was nobody in the Spylab either. What there was, however, was an enormous funnel that had descended from the ceiling; an immense circle in the barn roof had been pulled into a point towards the floor. It floated there like an enormous metal ice-cream cone. The point of the cone hovered a few feet above the floor in the middle of the barn sized Spylab. The top of the cone, where the ice cream should be, was suspended beneath a giant disk of open night air, and swirling in the hole in the roof was a whirlwind of grass and wool. Suddenly the wind dropped, the circling debris dropped down into the funnel and all at once the night sky was visible to Janey, standing below.

Janey gasped. She'd never seen a sky like it. It was so black it was as though there was nothing there at all – just a void, as pitch dark and empty as the pupil of an eye. Across it lay a spangled road, glittering white with little swirls of misty cloud trailing along it. It looked to Janey like a path to the heavens. 'Wow,' she whispered.

'It's the Milky Way,' said her father's voice. Janey jumped. She'd been completely lost and open-mouthed with awe at the beauty of the night sky, but now she focused on the direction from which her father had spoken. He was leaning on the railing at the door high up in the wall where the SPIral staircase led in from the outside. At his side stood Chloe, smiling at Janey's wonderment. 'It's amazing, isn't it?' she said. 'Like you could just jump out into the galaxy.'

Janey smiled back. 'It's so . . . beautiful!'

'So you see why I like it here,' said Abe, guiding Chloe down the stairs. She looked much better than before, but still slightly shaky on her thin legs, like a new-born foal. They crossed the barn and stood before Janey, Abe looking directly into her eyes. 'It's everything I could wish for. You see why I stay?'

Janey nodded slowly. 'Yes, I do see. It's wonderful. But I'm not sure . . .'

'What, Janey?' he prompted gently.

'I'm still not sure you'll be happy, giving up spying for good.'

'Ah.' Abe frowned for a moment, his eyes flashing towards Chloe and back to Janey. 'Well, spying isn't everything, you know.'

Chloe looked at their father uncomfortably, as if she'd just done or was about to say something wrong. Finally, after a struggle with herself, she spoke. 'At least you got to be a Spylet, Janey. I just get to be . . . this.' She spread her thin hands wide, looking pathetically at Janey.

That girl could really do with a Wower, thought Janey. It would be good for her to experience the blast of invincibility that surged through Janey's limbs whenever the Wower's robotic hands and miraculous droplets got to work on her. 'You're not so bad,' she said gently. Suddenly she had a thought. 'I could train Chloe, Dad! Then she could be a Spylet! For a bit, at least.'

Abe's eyes sparked briefly. 'I'm sure Chloe would make an excellent Spylet. After all, it's in her genes every bit as much as it is in yours, Janey. But that doesn't fit in with my plans, does it?'

'Suppose not,' said Janey slowly. Her twin raised her eyebrows in a gesture that said to Janey: 'thanks for trying'. She gave her a small half-smile back, then looked up as the high door in the wall was suddenly thrown back on its hinges.

'I almost forgot!' Abe took Janey's hand quickly, and led her across the Spylab floor. 'There's another important person who won't need to stay behind any more if you're not doing any spying, isn't there? I thought you'd feel more comfortable if you were here together.'

'M -Mum?' Janey was so delighted she thought she might burst. So he hadn't forgot about her mother after all! In fact, quite the opposite: he'd gone back home, explained everything to Jean, and persuaded her to join them all in Australia. 'Fantastic!'

She jumped on to the bottom step excitedly, ready to vault up them to give her mother a huge hug, but the person who stepped through the door was not her mother. The platform at the top of the stairs creaked loudly as a large body, flamboyantly dressed in a vast hat with dangling corks and a bouffant yellow sundress, wriggled through the narrow door.

'Hullll-lo Australia!' shouted G-Mamma as if she was addressing a capacity crowd at a stadium. 'Yo, spinny twinnies and your spy-licious daddy-o. G- Mamma's in da house!'

And Janey, quelling the initial stab of disappointment that it wasn't her mother at the top of the stairs, threw back her head and laughed aloud. Her friends and most of her family were there with her – her father, her new twin, Alfie, and now G-Mamma. She didn't need to worry about spies disappearing. They were all *appearing*, right next to her. Her dad was doing everything he could to make her feel comfortable, at ease, wanted. And pretty soon, she was sure, her mum would be there too, and the family could start out. Together. Properly.

Chapter 13 Sheep to keep

By breakfast the next morning, G-Mamma had commandeered Bert's little set of rooms at the end of the building as her own and eaten most of the contents of the humongous double-fronted fridge. She'd also given Janey a tight smile as the Spylet took out a portable Wower-head she found in G-Mamma's case. 'Oh yes. That. Thought you might like to get out of that SPIsuit,' she said, with a delicate wrinkle of her nose.

Janey had got so used to the suit that she'd stopped thinking about it, but now that G-Mamma mentioned it she realised she had been encased in silver Lycra for a very long time. She'd even slept in it the previous night, after Chloe had taken her back to her room, as Abe had been quite insistent that there wasn't enough water for her to de-Wow. 'Dad didn't want us to use too much water.'

'I won't tell. Use my shower,' replied G-Mamma grandly, ignoring the harrumphing sounds from across the table where Bert was pretending to read the paper. Every so often his eyes would dart to G-Mamma and fix on her in a puzzled fashion, as he tried to work out how this strange woman had managed to winkle him out of his home and into a camp bed in one of the barns in less time than it would take him to shear a sheep.

Janey noticed the affronted noises and decided not to offend Bert any further. 'I'll do it later,' she said quietly, 'and for now I can just borrow some of Chloe's clothes again.'

'Fine.' G-Mamma swiped the last two pieces of toast and buttered then lavishly, then sandwiched her entire meal between them. Janey, Alfie and Bert watched, amazed, as the great chunk of breakfast headed for G-Mamma's mouth.

'G-Mamma,' said Janey, pointing at the sandwich, 'did you know you've still got the plate in there?'

At this the SPI:KE stopped, peered into the small loaf before her and extracted the white crockery from it. 'Well, there's a thing. Could have broken my teeth! And did you ever see such a wonderful set of gnashers?' She curled back her lips at Bert, who threw down his paper and backed away from the table as if a gargoyle had just come to life in front of him.

'Crazy Sheila,' he muttered to himself as he left the room. 'What kind of name is G-Mamma, anyway?'

'Cheek!' said G-Mamma loudly. 'What kind of name is Bert?'

'Actually, he's got a point.' Janey carried plates over to the sink, where Chloe was elbow deep in suds. 'He doesn't know any of us are spies, so we're all using our normal names. Perhaps you should use your other name too?'

G-Mamma burped extravagantly. 'What other name?'

'You know, your normal name,' said Janey. 'This is my normal name.'

Alfie spoke suddenly. He'd been so quiet that Janey had almost forgotten he was there. 'Normal name, not spy name,' he said tersely. 'Alfie Halliday, not Halo. Janey, not Blonde.'

'Oh.' G-Mamma stroked her chins thoughtfully. 'I see. Soooooo . . . How about you call me Rosie from now on, but just in front of Bert? Bertie Bert-Bert Botty-Bert . . .'

Janey threw some soap suds at her. 'Don't, G-Mamma. He's actually quite nice. And he loves his animals.'

'Aah, how sweet,' drawled Alfie sarcastically. 'I'm going to go look for Abe.' He scraped back his chair and drifted out of the room before Janey had a chance to ask if he'd wait for her.

'And I'm going to do some laundry.' Chloe put away the last of the breakfast dishes. 'Shall I wash your SPIsuit, Janey?'

Janey looked down at it, surprised. She'd never really thought about how it stayed clean – just assumed that all that jumping in and out of the Wower kept it looking good. It was strange that she shouldn't even think about it, while Chloe was mumsy enough to actually wash. Sometimes they weren't terribly alike   at all. Janey nodded quickly. 'I'll bring it in to you in a minute.'

As soon as Chloe had disappeared to the lean- to housing the laundry at the back of the house, Janey turned to G-Mamma. 'Are you OK?'

'Me?' G-Mamma blinked her huge blue eyes owlishly. 'Me smee? Of course! Never better. Never better in a sweater. Loving all this hot weather. Hot weather, all together. A rap! A new rap!'

She leaped up and shimmied around the kitchen, not even stopping when Bert passed the back door, shook his head slowly and wondered off with an aggrieved expression.

'Yeah!
G-Mamma never felt be-tter. Never better in her swea-ter. G's loving this hot wea-ther. Hot weather, all toge-ther.

'Join in, Janey baby, Janey the babe babe, babe the Janey Zany, Blondey blonde Jane Jane baby . . .'

Janey put a hand on her SPI:KE's arm before she could draw another breath and start raving all over again. 'Erm, calm down, G-Mamma. I think you might have a bit of sunstroke or jet lag or something.'

'Nonsense!' G-Mamma threw open a cupboard and rifled wildly through the packages. 'Just hungry, that's all. Where are their *doughnuts*?'

Janey reached into the bread bin and passed G-Mamma the remains of a Victoria sponge that Bert had made the previous day. 'Here. Could you listen while you're eating?' G-Mamma nodded enthusiastically so Janey carefully closed the back door. 'There's something

109

funny going on. Dad's really intent on giving up spying. Chloe's obviously not very well; I've even seen him carrying her around at night. And there's other stuff too. Chloe disappeared while she was brushing my hair the other night, and I had this horrible dream with my dad saying he despised me, but I wasn't even asleep! Trouble sort of brought me round by jumping on my lap. Alfie's acting all weird, like he's too cool to be friends with me any more, and I . . . I miss my mum.'

'Your mum's fine. Probably doing a pensioners' weaving course in Bognor Regis or something fascinating.'

'Well, I still miss her. And Dad hasn't even mentioned her yet.'

'Blah blah blah,' said G-Mamma, playing a pretend violin. 'She'll be here soon enough, boring us all stupid.'

Janey stopped and stared. G-Mamma had never made any secret of the fact that she didn't like her old colleague Gina's new Jean Brown persona, but she'd never been quite so openly hostile about her before. Taking a deep breath, she changed tack. 'Well, what about the hair then?'

G-Mamma felt under her cork hat quickly. 'What? Wrong colour? What's wrong with it?'

'No, the sheep-mixed-with-human hair.'

'Oh, that! No,' said the SPI:KE, shoving her hat down hard and heading out of the back door, 'I was wrong about that. It's, you know, that thing. The thing that Abe said.'

'Angora? But you said it was probably human. So it is rabbit?' Janey scooted along behind G-Mamma, finally resorting to her Fleet-fleet as the woman popped fat little wheels out of the bottom of her boots and roller-skated over to the distant paddocks.

'Yip. Angora, that's the stuff. I got the wrong hoppy little beastie. When you thought I said "hair", I really meant "hare". H–A–R–E. Easy mistake to make. Rabbit. Grab it. Grab it, it's rabbit. Or is it hare? Oh, hare we go . . .

'Grab it, it's rabbit (dunph dunph dunph dunph)
Snare it, it's hare (dunph dunph dunph dunph)

Eat it, it's meat it's . . . (dunph dunph dunph dunph) Going nowhere! (dunph dunph dunph dunph)

Janey slowed down as Bert became visible in the distance. 'G-Mamma, that's kind of sick . . .'

'Oh, good lord above, I mean below – where is the lord in Australia?' G-Mamma swivelled her wheels into a sliding stop. 'What the spiky SPI:KE is that?'

Janey looked to where G-Mamma, wrinkling her nose beneath her vast sunglasses, was pointing. 'It's Maddy the sheep, with Trouble on her back. I think Twubs keeps the sun off her bald spot.'

Before G-Mamma said anything, Bert shouted over to them. 'When you two ladies have finished gossiping, there are two hundred sheep to groom over here.'

Alfie, Abe, Bert and Chloe were all busy with curry combs, brushing burrs out of the silky hair of the whole of

111

the flock apart from Maddy. G-Mamma inspected her nails in an obvious fashion. 'ONE, I am not getting my hands mucked up in there, and TWO, I don't take orders from you, Berty Bert-Bert.'

'He's right, Rosie,' called Abe from the other side of the paddock. 'All these sheep need to look great before we ship them off this afternoon. They need to be there by sundown, or the deal's off. All hands-on deck.'

'Now him, I take orders from,' said G-Mamma pointedly. She picked up a brush from the pile near the gate and headed over to where Abe was working.

Bert pulled his hat further down his brow and moved on to another sheep. Janey watched G-Mamma for a moment, then took a comb for herself, but before grooming the nearest silk-woolled sheep she turned to Maddy and ran the comb across her bedraggled coat.

'There you go, girl,' she said kindly. 'Can't have you all left out, can we?' She spruced up Maddy's head and even tried to give her a Trouble-style quiff. The sheep rewarded her with a loud paaaa.

'She's calling me,' said a voice in Janey's ear.

Her father was standing right behind her, grinning. 'Don't worry about that one too much. We're not selling her.'

'I just wanted her to feel nice,' said Janey quietly. 'And talking of which–' Abe put his arm around Janey's shoulders, a little awkwardly from his great height – 'a little birdie tells me that *you'd* feel a lot nicer if your mother was here. Well, I hadn't planned on getting her over yet – there's such a lot to explain to a non-spy as she is now. But if it means that much to you, I'll bring Jean here as soon as possible.'

Janey squeezed Abe hard. 'It does! It does mean that much to me! And it means a lot to you too, doesn't it?'

Her father twinkled his film-star grin at her. 'More than you could know. It's the final piece of our jigsaw, isn't it?'

'All our family together,' agreed Janey. She could hardly contain her glee, and seeing G-Mamma looking at her across the paddock, she treated her SPI:KE to a huge grin and a thumbs-up. Chloe waved too, with a tired smile in Janey's direction. The family together. Everything was going to be just fine.

And for the rest of the day, everything was. The whole group of them worked courageously through the blistering heat, combing and brushing and beautifying the flock until they gleamed like little Palomino horses. Grinning so widely that his face resembled a cracked leather sofa, Bert ushered the sheep on to two enormous trucks with the help of Trouble, who fancied himself as a bit of a sheep-cat and actually managed to do quite a good job of rounding up any sheep that strayed from the edges of the pack. Only ninety or so remained behind, surplus to requirements. At 5 p.m. Abe got into one truck and followed Bert out along the farm track, a weathered arm from each cab signalling farewell to the workers.

Tired, but pleased with what they'd achieved, Janey, Alfie, Chloe and G-Mamma made their way back to the house. After a quick wash-up, during which time Janey finally managed to change into some jeans again, they had tea – a hasty barbecue on the back veranda. It suited everyone just fine. Soon afterwards, however, Alfie started to look rather green.

'Are you OK, Alfie?' said Janey.

He put down the remainder of his pork sausage. 'Erm, not really. Maybe these sausages weren't quite cooked. I feel a bit sick.'

G-Mamma was also an odd shade of grey beneath her suntan and layers of blusher. 'You could be right – I don't feel quite the thing myself. I think I'll turn in for the night. No disturbing my beauty sleep, you hear?'

'No way – you need all the help you can get,' said Alfie.

'Rude dude!' retorted G-Mamma.

Alfie smirked as Janey stared at him. He *was* being rude, and not even under his breath. 'Truth hurts,' he said in a loud voice.

'Alfie . . .' But Janey turned to Chloe as she heard a noise. Her twin was also paling under the stark glare of the kitchen bulb. 'You don't look so good either, Chloe.'

Chloe shook her head. 'Bed for me as well. You go in the spare room next door, Janey. I'll brush your hair for you first, if you like.'

'No, I'm fine, thanks.'

'I'm off too,' said Alfie. 'You and Trouble can finish those off, if you're not having a girly makeover.' He pointed to the offending sausages and staggered off, clutching his stomach.

'I feel fine. I wonder why the bangers haven't affected me? Anyway, looks like it's just you and me, Twubs,' said Janey, peering out into the fading light. One thing Janey had noticed in Australia was that it got dark very quickly – no long dusky evenings; just light one minute, and dark the next, almost as if a switch had been flicked. There was still no sign of her father and Bert returning with the trucks, and she was glad it was them and not her having to drive the great lorries back along the farm tracks in the blackness.

Janey was just throwing the sausages away, not even daring to give them to Trouble, when the phone rang. She skipped to it, hoping for a friendly voice, but the person on the other end was anything but. 'Get that mongrel Rownigan, will ya!'

Janey nearly dropped the phone. It felt hot with the anger pouring down it. 'I'm s-sorry, Mr Rownigan's out delivering sheep at the moment.'

'Well, you tell him as soon as he gets back that those sheep of his are useless,' barked the man. 'They've all run off. Can't find a single one of them! He won't be getting a blasted cent – you can tell him from me.'

The man banged down the receiver just as Abe and Bert came through the door. 'Oh no. That was your customer. He says all the sheep have run off and you can't have your money.'

Bert exploded. 'Well, that's his fault! If he hasn't got dogs that can keep a couple of hundred sheep together, then he's a fool to himself! Let me get him on the phone . . .' 'Leave it, Bert,' said Abe quietly. He looked . . .not exactly worried, but rather more as if he was trying to work out some fractions, thought Janey. 'We can't do anything now. I'll sort it out later. In the morning. He'll have his sheep.'

'How, exactly?' said Bert, mopping his brow with a great red handkerchief. 'We only left ninety behind, and he wants two-twenty.'

'I'll manage,' Abe snapped.

'Well, it'll be an early start,' Bert said eventually. 'I'll hit the sack.'

Janey put her hand on her dad's arm. 'I'll help, Dad. I'm not tired. I'll go and comb sheep or whatever.'

Abe rubbed a hand across his face. 'Just go to bed, Janey.'

'But don't you want—'

'No, I don't!' Abe drew in a deep breath, then looked at Janey apologetically. 'No, thank you, Janey. Sorry. There's nothing anyone can do right now. I'll work it out myself. Get yourself off to bed.'

Janey kissed his cheek quietly and stepped into the corridor. When she turned to say goodnight, her father was staring after her, that same odd look of calculation on his face. 'Night, Dad,' she said. He just nodded. Janey walked away, and after a moment she heard a footfall and the back-door swing to as Abe went back outside.

He was tired, she told herself as she crept past the room where Alfie slept. He was worried about the sheep contract. She gave herself as many reasons as she could why Abe should be so short with her, almost unpleasant, but in the end her spy instincts rattled her sufficiently to make her stick her hand through Chloe's open door, grab the Wower-head from her bag and keep walking, or rather creeping, out of the front door.

Something was not right. Her dad was just being peculiar. Maybe years of spying had made him extra-secretive, but he didn't need to hide things from Janey. He was in more trouble than he was allowing her to know. That message on the email hadn't just been a general warning, Janey was sure. He needed Jane Blonde. There was something going on, and she was going to find out what.

Chapter 14 Nifty nostrils

S linking through the shadows, Janey pressed herself against the walls of the Spylab. The familiar square of light illuminated the courtyard, and once more the wind was creating a froth of flotsam and jetsam that swirled around Janey's head. It was so gusty that she found it difficult to move along the wall to the window to take a peek inside the lab, but after much pushing and gasping, she finally made it. Had she been Wowed already, Janey might have been tempted just to hold her Ultra-gogs up to the windowpane to register what was going on inside. As it was, she was just in jeans and a scratchy wool jumper that Chloe had offered her, so after a moment or two Janey poked her nose above the window sill, and just at that moment the wind subsided a little so that she didn't have to struggle against it and risk making any tell-tale noises.

It was no great surprise to see Abe inside, dressed in safety goggles and a white lab coat. Janey thought at first that he was examining at the sharp tip of the metal cone, which was once more poking down towards the floor. When she looked again, however, she could see that his lips were moving. She followed the angle of his face; it led up, past the cone, to the top of the metal staircase leading up to the little platform on which G-Mamma had appeared just a short time ago, through the door from the outside where the SPIral staircase stood. It wasn't empty. Abe was definitely talking to someone.

It was Alfie and Chloe. Not ill. Not suffering with food poisoning. Looking completely fine.

Janey slumped back against the wall, swallowing hard. The stab of betrayal seemed to go up through her stomach, piercing her diaphragm and her lungs and making its way under her ribcage and straight into her heart. How could her father refuse her help and send her to bed, yet arrange to meet Alfie and Chloe immediately afterwards? How could her best friend and her twin pretend to be sick from sausages and then sneak out behind her back? How could they all leave her out like that?

Barely able to look, yet oddly incapable of stopping herself, Janey peeked over the window sill once more. Alfie and Chloe had circled the blanket-covered object on the platform and were walking down the stairs. Behind them the door was opening. Janey wouldn't have been at all surprised to see G-Mamma appear on the platform – the final betrayal – but just at that moment there was a plaintive bleat from just inside the main doorway and all three pairs of eyes inside the Spylab barn swivelled round to focus on whatever had made the noise. Janey ducked quickly.

'Paaaaaaa,' came the mournful cry again.

Maddy! The call sounded distressed, but she felt unwilling to help. She was neither wanted nor needed, it seemed. And though that wasn't Maddy's fault, Janey was

119

so angry that she didn't even particularly care about her favourite sheep. She heard heavy footsteps walking over to the doorway and then a sharp 'Paa!' from Maddy as someone – Abe – clearly grabbed her and started dragging her towards the cone.

Right then, Janey knew just how Maddy felt. Left out. Friendless. Picked on. The feeling of hurt sat inside her chest like a heavy, undigested supper. She only wished she could cough it up and get rid of it. It felt far too much like the old Janey to be at all comfortable. And suddenly Janey realised something. It *was* like the old Janey. The old Janey had not discovered her spy instincts, and now this nervous energy was masking them, sitting directly over the point under her sternum where she felt things most keenly. She took a few deep breaths to calm herself, and listened to her subconscious. It held her back, stopped her walking into the barn and confronting everyone. The only reason they'd go behind her back was to protect her from something . . . wasn't it? What else could they be up to? And with poor Maddy, hunched up like the victim in a ring of school bullies . . .

She badly needed to Wow. Reaching into her pocket, Janey veered off towards the first sheep pen.

A creaking tap stand stood at the end of each long water trough, and it was to the first of these that Janey now ran. The portable Wower-head she'd taken from her bag screwed on to the tap after a little wiggling and pushing. Unfortunately it was very low down, just above waist height for Janey, but she quickly up ended four of the metal water troughs to create a Wower cubicle, crouched under the dripping faucet and turned the tap on.

Instantly Janey's mood lifted as the enhancing power of the Wower went to work. A small metallic hand detangled her sticky, greasy hair and smoothed it into her trademark slick blonde ponytail. Her long limbs, aching from grooming several dozen sheep, were soothed and wrapped in the wisps of fresh silver Lycra that flowed out of the Wower-head, and suddenly her vision cleared as her Ultra-gogs were popped on to her nose. She was Blonde again. It felt great.

Janey tipped the troughs back into position urgently and ran on, little knowing that she had left behind a luxuriant patch of grass that would thrive through the toughest droughts and mystify farmers for decades to come. Fleet-footed and Blonded, in just a few moments she managed to make it to the far paddock where the sheep had been corralled that afternoon. 'Weird,' said Janey, looking around. It seemed that the customer's sheep weren't the only ones to have run away. None of the ninety they'd kept back were here either. The field was completely empty.

'Long distance,' said Janey, instructing her Ultra-gogs.

It made no difference; she turned fully through three hundred and sixty degrees, trying to spot sheep in the bush, in the outer-lying paddocks, even on the neighbouring farmer's land several miles away – but even though she could definitely see the odd one, they were not the distinctive long-haired sheep of Dubbo Seven. She sighed, but just as she turned back to her original position, she happened to look down.

At her feet was a little slick of the vomit-like dissolved sheep food. Janey knelt down to inspect it more closely, noticing as she did so that there were lots of pools, dotted all over the field. Once again, she felt that sharp reminder in her chest that something wasn't right. She bent over further to inspect the puddle. It certainly did have a strange smell . . .

Just as Janey inhaled, she felt a very strange sensation in her nose, like an insect had been sheltering up there and had just decided to move. She suddenly wanted to sneeze, desperately, but even as she straightened her shoulders and went to put her head back, the odd feeling intensified. With considerable horror, Janey felt something descend from her nose.

It was a long piece of string. All the way from Janey's left nostril it ran, unfurling right down to the ground and dangling for a moment or so in the sticky mound at Janey's feet, before rolling back up and making its way back inside her nostril. 'That is disgusting,' said Janey aloud, planning to shout very loudly at G-Mamma the next time she could get a word in edgeways. 'I don't ever want to use a SPInal cord again!'

The gadget was gross but effective, however. As Janey breathed in deeply, trying to force down the bile that was rising in her throat, threatening to add a fresh little pile of Spylet-sick to the other patches of gloop on the ground, she felt a buzzing in the other nostril. The buzzing became more insistent – the beetly insect had now become a bee, wedged inside her nose. To Janey's revulsion, something else now drooped from her nose, but only as far as her top lip this time. She steeled herself, reached up her Girl-gauntleted hand and pulled.

To her amazement, a tiny printout had been issued from her nose. Janey moved it across the palm of her glove with her thumb, careful not to touch it, and zoomed in with her Ultra-gogs. The tiny ticker tape had two pieces of information on it. '"1. Sheep DNA",' read Janey. '"Makes sense. 2. Jane Blonde DNA". Right.' That also made sense. The SPInal cord had identified her own DNA from the inside of her nose (which she tried not to think about too much) and then the DNA of the sheep from their contact with the melted food. It was perfectly logical, but it didn't help her much.

There didn't seem to be much else she could do at this point. Janey had one last Ultra-gog search for sheep, but she was already resolved to going back to the Spylab to confront her father. Why was he keeping her out of things and being so secretive? Why involve Alfie and Chloe but not her? It wasn't fair, and now she'd calmed down enough to face him she'd ask him outright. Just as she was turning back towards the house, the view finder in her Ultra-gogs shifted suddenly. Janey whipped her head around. Sure enough, there were two dark shadows in the next field. and as one of the shadows extended a long, ghostly hand to the other they merged into a distorted and hideous monster with a grotesque bloated head.

Someone, or something, was climbing out of Janey's eSPIdrills hole. A bubble of fear bobbed up Janey's windpipe, and she had to swallow hard to stop a squeak of alarm escaping. Then her spy instincts took over. Ignoring the patches of slimy gloop all over the field, she kept low and started to crawl.

Chapter 15 Nosy neighbours

Janey shuffled forward until her nose touched the bottom rung of the fence. The bubble-headed monster was sliding away from the eSPIdrills hole, dragging its long, lumpy tail behind it. 'Come on, Blonde,' said Janey under her breath. 'You've tackled worse than this.'

Pushing off from the knees, she launched herself under the fence and got to her feet, ready to pounce. But as she propelled herself forward she heard a familiar voice complaining vehemently: 'I'm just too *weak*, Maisie! Let me dangle here. Come back and get me later, and bring some food.'

Then, to Janey's amazement, Alfie's mother's voice boomed out of the bubble head. 'Rosie, I know you haven't been fed in a few days, but it still hasn't made you light enough for me to drag any more! I won't leave you here. Push!'

Janey ran forward and grabbed G-Mamma's other arm. 'Mrs H! G-Mamma, what are you doing down here in the paddock? Use your feet to jump,' she said to her SPI:KE, who had flopped on to the ground with only her head and shoulders poking out of the hole.

'W- what?' said G-Mamma feebly.

'Good idea, Janey.' Mrs Halliday braced herself at the edge of the tunnel. 'You've been Wowed, Rosie. Goodness knows you spent long enough in the Wower. Bang your feet against the side, and the detonation will push you out.'

'Oh,' said G-Mamma, sounding very vague. 'OK, Halo. Watch out then.'

She thumped her feet against the earthen walls of the tunnel; there was a dull *thwump*, and suddenly all three of them rocketed across the paddock and careered into a fence post. 'There! That's better.' G- Mamma smiled blearily before her head slumped back on to her arms. 'Clever shoes.' She was wearing Janey's eSPIdrills.

'What's the matter with her?' Janey had never seen her SPI:KE so wishy-washy. 'And what are you doing here?'

Mrs Halliday removed the SPIFFIG, looking quite formidable in a deep mauve SPIsuit with military- style decorations, and pulled G-Mamma upright. 'I found her locked in her Wower,' she said grimly. 'I was getting worried that I hadn't heard from Alfie so I went round to your Spylab to check everything was OK, and finally tracked Rosie down.'

'Someone shoved me in there and stuck a needle in my bottom!'

'They – what?' Janey herself had locked G- Mamma in the Wower, but this was obviously much more sinister than that. 'To sedate you?'

'I don't know,' wailed G-Mamma. 'I soon passed out with hunger though, I can tell you. Days I was in there. Days!'

126

'No, you can't have been.' Janey shook her head. 'You've been here, and you've been eating all day! You've done nothing *but* eat, apart from some really tasteless rapping.'

'What do you mean?' said Mrs Halliday sharply. 'She arrived last night, took over the overseer's rooms, ate all day like a starving woman and went to bed early.' She turned to her SPI:KE. Did you arrange to meet Mrs H here?'

G-Mamma shrugged, her lip wobbling tremulously. 'No. I don't know. I don't think so.'

'She may be hallucinating,' continued Maisie Halliday. 'She said you were the one who shoved her in the Wower.'

'I really didn't. Not this time.'

'Then I think we'd better go and investigate.'

As they walked across the paddocks, half carrying, and half dragging G-Mamma between them, they exchanged information. Having not heard from Alfie since his arrival in Australia, Mrs Halliday had become worried. She got to G-Mamma's Spylab to find egg wrappings and the bag from her own chocolate cake littered across the lab, then finally found the SPI:KE in the Wower. There'd also been a message from Solomon blinking on the computer screen. 'Here.' Mrs Halliday passed a colour printout to Janey.

'A speckly bird and a pair of kneecaps, inside Trouble's belly like he's just swallowed them,' said Janey, thinking quickly.

'I got it instantly.' Mrs Halliday paused to help G-Mamma over a stile. 'So did G-Mamma, I suppose.'

Janey nodded. 'I do too. The bird's a jay, with a pair of knees, inside Trouble: Jay. Knees. In Trouble. "Janey's in trouble." I'm not though. What does he mean?'

Mrs Halliday shrugged. 'Once I'd found Rosie we thought we'd better get here straight away. Of course, it would have been easier to travel by SPIral staircase, but the lift capsule seems to have got stuck at this end.'

'Oh no! I can see why G-Mamma would be so bleary. She must have arrived by SPIral – in fact, she definitely did, because she appeared on that platform behind the Spylab – but then she must have been Satisfied back home.'

'Well, the only thing we could think of – or rather, I could think of – was for Rosie to wear the eSPIdrills and me to sit on her shoulders with the longest SPIFFIG I could find over my head. I just hoped it would cover us both. It did, just about, but that was an extremely hazardous journey. Still, you're not in any danger, it seems.'

'No, but I'm glad you're here, Mrs H. I knew Dad was worried about something and wasn't letting on.' Janey sighed. 'He's being a bit odd. Like he's more worried about his sheep than he is about me. He doesn't seem himself.'

128

They were approaching the Spylab now, dragging G-Mamma behind them like a collapsed parachute. Propping her SPI:KE up against the side of the building, Janey beckoned to Mrs Halliday, and the Spylet and spy made their way to the window.

'There's Alfie!' His mother was just about to bound into the lab, but Janey held out a restrain- ing hand. Something very peculiar was happening inside.

Abe, Chloe and Alfie were positioning a small-wheeled cabinet – one of the half-dozen or so that lined the far wall of the lab – beneath the point of the metal cone suspended in the middle of the room. The cabinet had a floor and four sides (one with a small slot in it), but no top, and Janey could just make out the matted woolly head of Maddy inside it. Her heart went out to the poor creature, who was paaaaing madly. Janey put a finger to her lips to silence Mrs Halliday, then zoomed her Ultra-gogs to get a better view of what happened next.

Abe had turned away to face the bench top. Now he came back into view, plucking at something as though he were playing a small zither. But it wasn't an instrument, Janey realised quickly. It was a hairbrush – the very same hairbrush that Chloe had used to brush Janey's hair as she sat at her dressing table.

Janey watched as her father extracted a hair from the bristles, 'That's my hair,' she said to Mrs Halliday, puzzled as to why he would clean hairbrushes in the Spylab. In fact, why would he clean her hairbrush at all?

They both watched as Abe fed the hair carefully through the slit in the side of the cabinet containing Maddy. Then he nodded at Chloe, who was standing by one of the other counters. A crop of levers and pulleys that Janey had never noticed before bristled before Chloe and Alfie. Janey's twin pushed one of the levers downwards and then snapped on some ear defenders.

Feeling rather sick, Janey turned to Mrs Halliday. 'I've just realised something!' she squeaked as loudly as she dared. 'He's not using angora – or hare, as G- Mamma said. I *knew* she'd said human hair, and that's what he's using. And it isn't any old human hair – it's mine! That's why the SPInal cord said my DNA and the sheep's were mixed! Eugh, that is so revolting!'

'What's he doing?' gasped Mrs Halliday.

'I don't know! It's horrid! What . . . what's happening now?'

To Janey's amazement, the great cone of metal had started to turn. She'd thought it was solid at its tip but could see now that it wasn't. As the cone spun faster and faster, a great whirlwind of air began to form over it, a vast vortex, sucking in all the surrounding debris, bits of wool, tools that hadn't been anchored down, even Abe's mask from the top of his head. Janey and Mrs Halliday clung on to the window sill as the rush of air lifted them off their feet; they streamed out from the wall, hanging on only by the tips of their fingers. The clothes of the people inside the barn were being whipped around furiously, and Chloe's hair had twisted into a strange pretzel shape on top of her head, knotted around the ear defenders, but Janey could see now that she, Alfie and Abe were weighted to the floor by thick iron bars that held them down like great metal sandals.

But the strangest thing of all was what was happening to Maddy. Positioned directly under the point of the cone in her little open-top cage, the sheep had been lifted clean off her feet. Strands of the golden hair Abe had fed into the cage now glinted on her pink and otherwise hairless back; then she was rising up through the air, bleating furiously, till an enormous slurping sound signalled that the poor animal was fully suctioned on to the point of the cone. Maddy now dangled several feet in the air, stuck in a little lump to the bottom of the sleek metallic cone, like the gumball in a Screwball. Most of her back had disappeared into the hole, so that Janey could see instantly why she had her peculiar monk-like wool pattern – the wool on her back had just been sucked off and up into the vortex, together with Janey's own hair – and Maddy's legs flopped around, buffeted this way and that by the small hurricane in the lab.

'They can't do that! It's cruel!" she screamed over the roar of the wind.

'Look, Janey!' Mrs Halliday, face contorted by the gale, pointed up to the sky above the vortex.

Jancy couldn't believe what she was seeing. The metal cone was rattling and shaking with such ferocity that it must surely come away at any moment from the delicate wiring that tethered it to the ceiling. The whirlwind above the cone was spiralling insanely, sucking everything in with its grasping, rasping breath . . . and then suddenly there was a deathly pause, the wind changed direction, something popped up, spat out by the vortex, and flew out of sight behind the barn.

It was a sheep. A golden straight-haired sheep. Or, at least, it was partly a sheep. Only partly, because the other part, Janey realised with a jolt that made her think she too might part company with the sausages they'd eaten earlier, was something else. Someone else. It was a new sheep, somehow created from Maddy . . . and Jane Blonde's hair.

And when the vortex popped out another one, and then another, and another, until a whole stream of silky sheep were flying over the top of the barn like a flock of short-necked swans, Janey finally lost her grip on reality. She passed out, just as a spitting Spycat hurtled past them, fresh from the Wower in the paddock and now equipped with a bright beacon of a tail, yellow go-faster stripes the entire length of this body, blazing emerald eyes and a wickedly sharp hooked claw unfurled from his lion-like paw.

'Trouble,' murmured Janey, as her cat jumped into the barn with his sabre- claw poised for a fight.

Chapter 16 The cinderella defect

Janey came to with a small circle of anxious faces peering down at her. The wind had dropped away completely, and she was able to hear Maddy's sad bleating once more. She could also hear a hissed argument between Alfie and his mother, along the lines of 'I never promised!' and 'That doesn't matter – I was worried about you!' Abe, meanwhile, was holding a squirming Trouble out in front of him, a firm brown hand in the scruff of the cat's neck. His other hand, Janey noticed quickly, was bleeding.

'Janey! Are you all right?' he asked.

She pointed to the deep cut across his wrist. 'Are you, Dad? Sorry. Trouble's very protective of me sometimes. He must have thought you had something to do with me fainting.'

Her father sighed as the others looked at him. 'Trouble was right. I did have something to do with you fainting! You saw what I've been doing. So did you, dear Maisie.'

'I did.' Mrs Halliday nodded sternly. 'It looks to me like you're splicing sheep genes together with your own daughter's hair. Crossing sheep with humans?' She shook her head, lips pursed.

'Ah, you don't approve,' said Abe with a small smile. 'I understand. It does seem a terrible use of my own daughter's genes. But it makes absolute sense. I sell a few

133

hundred of these sheep, and we're set up for life. We'll make a killing, and I can give up spying and settle down with my family. All of my family, and my friends,' he finished, with a dazzling smile at the Spylets and spies looking at him. 'Anyway, my discovery is a little better than simply mutating sheep genes. Come and look.'

Janey got to her feet, held up on either side by Alfie and Chloe, just as G-Mamma appeared from around the corner. She looked much perkier than she had earlier, when Mrs Halliday and Janey had left her slumped like an old mattress against a barn wall. 'Wait for me!' she carolled chirpily. 'I want to see this too.'

'You seem better, Rosie,' said Mrs Halliday. 'I thought you were too weak to move?'

G-Mamma rolled her eyes. 'I just needed *food*. Good job for me that old Bert's a bit of a baker. I just cleaned out the cake tin.'

'Speaking of Bert,' warned Abe, 'let's go before he gets up. I don't want him to know about this.'

With that, he led the phalanx of spies across the Spylab, past the cabinet containing Maddy (which Janey casually unlatched as she passed so that the sheep could skitter off across the floor) and over to the metal steps leading up to the SPIral staircase door. They followed him up the stairs – Janey first, then Halo and G-Mamma, with Alfie and Chloe bringing up the rear. Once they were all assembled on the platform, Abe pointed back to the metal cone.

'That, my dear friends, is my latest invention. As usual, I've borrowed from some existing technology, enhanced the process somewhat and created something very . . . special and very unusual. Nobody else must ever hear of this, do you understand?'

Janey nodded along with the others. She reached out to the rail around the platform to steady herself, in case the news was so monumental that she went wobbly again. After all, so far her father had discovered how to create new life from a different life form, and had uncloaked a method for immortality based on a cat's nine lives. This new development was likely to be something immense. Life-changing, perhaps.

Abe rubbed blood off the back of his hand. 'Plenty more where that came from. Now to the matter in hand. Some of you may have heard of Dolly the sheep?'

Mrs Halliday nodded. 'The clone?'

'The very same. A sheep that wasn't born of two parent sheep, but created by man – an exact copy of a sheep, living and breathing and solid, but completely artificial. Well, I've perfected the cloning process. I can clone sheep, not once but many, many times over, using the power of wind in a vortex to stir up the gene pool and create new life forms. I call it . . . the SPI- clone.'

'Like "cyclone"!' G-Mamma beamed. 'Oh, that is good! I'll be able to come up with some juicy-licious raps with that one.'

'Later, G-Mamma,' said Abe shortly. 'For now, I want you to look at this.'

He flung open the door behind him, and they all stepped through on to the external platform at the top of the SPIral staircase. Janey gasped. There in the paddock below them were a few dozen long-haired, blonde sheep, glowing like pink clouds as the sun seeped over the horizon.

'Cloned sheep. I just made them,' said Abe. 'But they are not true clones, because true clones would simply be carbon copies of the first sheep used, the ugly one. You'll see that these are far from ugly. Quite the opposite. I've told the industry that I used the very rare Andalusian mountain sheep to breed with, but the truth is there is no such sheep. That's a shame actually – with a proper original I could make really strong clones, perfect the process. But I created my sheep from scratch, using Bert's prize-winning merino. There, in the depths of the SPI-clone, the sheep's original genes merge with the newly introduced DNA– in this case, Janey's – to form a new blueprint: the long-haired sheep. And then I just push the button, and out pop as many as I need. And –' here he paused to smile proudly at Janey – 'this flock is the first of the dazzling Dubbo Seven Blonde variety – the first time we've used Jane Blonde's hair instead of Janey Brown's. They'll create a storm.'

At this, G-Mamma broke into spontaneous applause, and even Alfie ventured some praise, although in typical

Alfie-fashion it was fairly back- handed. 'Brilliant,' he said, nodding slowly. 'Sick, but brilliant.'

Janey looked down at the sheep in the pen beneath her. It was brilliant – every bit as clever as she might have expected of her genius father. She wanted to be pleased for him and congratulate him on his success and his cleverness, but somehow all she could think about was poor Maddy having her DNA sucked out of her on a nightly basis, so much so that it made her wool disappear, and that these odd-looking sheep were made partly from her own spy genes. Something about it made her stomach turn, and she could see from Mrs Halliday's face that her headmistress was also repulsed by the whole thing, though the others were all gazing admiringly at her father like a small Abe Appreciation Society.

Suddenly Janey thought of something. 'Why do you need to *keep* making them, Dad? You said a few hundred would make you your fortune. So why not stop at that? Then Maddy could just . . . I don't know, retire or whatever old, baldy sheep do.'

Abe turned to her with a penetrating stare. 'Good question, Blonde. You're quite right, of course. I've perfected the SPI-clone mechanism, but there's something I haven't got quite right yet. As I mentioned, cloning from the original would make much stronger copies. I can make a very reasonable copy with a very limited amount of DNA, but because it's limited, the lifespan of my sheep-clones is very short. Less than a day. In fact, they seem to

137

have what I call a "Cinderella" defect – just as the sun goes down, they. . . well, dissolve.'

'And that's why your customer's flock completely disappeared!' Janey gasped. 'When you said you'd "sort it out", you meant you'd make some more!'

Abe smiled proudly. 'Correct. And while I'm doing it, I'm trying to solve the Cinderella defect. I can't keep turning up with a new flock every morning. I intend to make as many sheep as I can – take over the market. The world! And then,' he added quickly, with a look at Janey's face, 'we can all retire and settle down together.'

'That gunk! It's not food at all, is it? Those little patches in the paddock are melted sheep!' Janey looked from her father to the sheep, unable to put words to her innermost thoughts. As ever, what her father was doing really was quite fascinating, totally unique, but this time there was something about it that she really didn't like.

Fortunately Mrs Halliday said it for her. 'Forgive me for saying this: I understand perfectly, of course, why you would want to create a safe life for yourself and for your family – I've done very much the same myself, retraining as a headmistress. But isn't this a little . . . unethical?'

There was a long pause as Abe considered this. Finally he nodded. 'I expect it is. To normal mortals it probably would seem that way, and certainly the newspapers were full of discussion on the ethics of cloning when Dolly the sheep appeared. But if the *right* person has all the information I've already formed new life with the

Crystal Clarification process, and saved life through the nine-life bubble. Is either of those things "ethical"? Probably not. But it doesn't matter. And . . . I think I am that person.'

Janey stared for a moment at the glint of steel in her father's soft brown eyes. 'Dad,' she said softly, 'why didn't you just ask me for some hair? I would have given it to you. Or use Chloe's? You're our dad. We would have helped you.'

Chloe gave a slight nod, watching Abe a little fearfully as he stood, silent, choosing his words carefully. 'So many good questions, Blonde,' he said at length. 'Good spy work. Why not use Chloe's hair? Chloe, who's right here with me? Well, her hair is so fine and lank, it wouldn't make very good wool.' Chloe's lip wobbled, but Abe ignored her. 'Yours is stronger – even when it's Brown hair. And now you're Jane Blonde, and it's more powerful and glorious than ever.'

'But why . . . why didn't you just ask me, instead of getting hairs off my SPI-buys box and pulling them out of the hairbrush. That's why you kept wanting to brush my hair, isn't it, Chloe?'

Abe huffed out a great sigh as Chloe nodded, now sobbing softly. Gently, he took Janey's shoulders in his enormous hands, damp with sweat from the strain of explaining everything to his beloved daughter. 'I should have. I know I can trust you. You come the minute I say I need your help. You sacrifice everything for me. You'll do whatever it takes to save me and your family,' he said gently, smiling down at her. 'But I wanted to be sure I had perfected everything before involving you. I've done it before – turned up and disturbed your life, embroiled you in all sorts of danger, then walked away and left you to deal with it. I wanted to be sure. This time I wanted to be absolutely sure that we would never need to be separated . . . again.'

He looked around at the gathered spies, gazing at Alfie, Chloe and finally Janey, who he gathered up in an enormous embrace. Of course. That's why he'd been worried and unable to tell her. He wanted them to be together properly this time. He hadn't become head of his own spy organisation without having a heap of determination alongside his massive creativity and inventing genius, and he had vowed to sort all this out himself before bothering her with the details.

Squashing down the globule of discontent that was bobbing in her gullet, Janey smiled cheerily. 'It's really very clever, Dad. But look, the sun's nearly up. Bert will be waking in an hour or so. Hadn't we better get back to the house before he suspects anything?'

Her words seemed to diffuse the slight air of tension. 'You're right as ever, Janey,' said Abe, putting his arm around her shoulders. 'I expect we could all do with some sleep. Although it will only be a bit – good job we spies are made of stern stuff! Alfie, why don't you show your mum to your room? Chloe, you can sort Janey out, can't you?'

140

Janey's twin beamed at her. 'Yes! Come on, Janey. We can be all sisterly and chat under the sheets.'

'Sure.' Janey smiled back at her. It was nice to see a grin lighting up Chloe's sallow face. 'If Trouble can kip down on the end of the bed too.'

Thus organised, everyone but Abe trooped down the SPIral staircase, and he waved to them before heading back through the door to the lab. Janey fended off a yawn as they crossed the packed earth to the house, and held up a hand to Mrs Halliday and Alfie as they disappeared into their room. 'See you in the morning. In about an hour. Goodnight, G-Mamma.'

The twins stumbled into Chloe's room; Janey ached with tiredness, and for the first time she seemed more fatigued than Chloe. She stared in the mirror as Chloe climbed into the enormous bed and Trouble hopped up on to the duvet, the yawn that had been building up for a few minutes finally bursting out and splitting her face right across the middle. She giggled at her reflection, but even as she did so she heard the same whispering voice sneak into her brain. 'Blonde, I despise you!' rumbled her father's voice.

'What *is* that?'

Chloe threw back the duvet. 'What?'

'I keep thinking I hear Dad say he hates me!' said Janey.

'You must be very tired,' said Chloe slowly. 'Your mind's playing tricks on you. Of course he doesn't hate you!'

Janey shook her head quickly. It was ridiculous. She'd just seen her father, and he was very proud of her and her spy instincts. Chloe was right – tiredness must be getting to her. Firmly wishing she could leap into a Wower, Janey clambered into bed, yawning again. She patted Trouble on the head. 'What are you lying on, Twubs? A little cat duvet?'

Trouble was lying on his own little white quilt, silky and gleaming against the tawny glow of his fur. Janey looked at it more closely. It was a handkerchief or, to put it more accurately, it was a Wowed tissue, like the stack Alfie had stored in his drawers. Janey shrugged. Maybe it *was* Alfie's. She hauled the duvet over herself.

Her twin's solemn grey eyes were fixed on her. 'Goodnight, Janey,' said Chloe softly.

'Mmm, night,' said Janey. 'I'm sleepy.'

'It's been a long night,' agreed Chloe. 'Sleep well.'

And just to be sure she did, Janey pressed gently on the ring she was still wearing under the bedclothes. The duvet straightened as the USSR's forcefield anchored itself around Janey's body, and as the dawn chorus of parrots and cockatoos reached a crescendo, Janey fell into a deep sleep.

Chapter 17 Hands, knees and bumpsamaises

The bedroom was empty when Janey's eyes opened again a few hours later: no Chloe, no Trouble and no strange ghostly voices talking to her from the dressing table. Sunshine was radiating through the thin cotton curtains, so Janey threw the blankets to one side and swung her legs, still clad in SPIsuit silver, on to the polished wooden floor.

She needed to grab a pair of jeans and a top to get out of her SPIsuit, so she pulled open one of Chloe's enormous wooden drawers and rifled through her clothes. She'd just found a pair of sawn-off jeans when she noticed something white, scrunched into a corner of the drawer. 'The handkerchief!' It was clearly the one Trouble had been sleeping on last night, as there was an enormous slash through the middle of it from his sabre-claw – there must have been a tussle to get him off it. Janey grinned: Trouble was pretty possessive when he was particularly fond of something, and he'd obviously become very partial to the hanky. She'd have to apologise to Chloe on her cat's behalf . . .

In the cut-off jeans and a clean T-shirt, Janey made her way to the big airy kitchen, wondering if she might be too late for breakfast. She needn't have worried – all her friends, even Bert, were still sitting around the table. Only

Abe was missing from the picture, as he often seemed to be in the morning (though Janey now understood why).

'Good morning, Janey, do join us,' said Mrs Halliday briskly. 'Sit. It's time for breakfast.' She clapped her hands efficiently like she did before school assembly and pointed Janey towards a chair.

As directed, Janey sat in the chair next to Alfie. He grunted vaguely in her direction and sank his teeth into some thickly buttered toast. 'Thought you were all getting some beauty sleep,' he said eventually between bites. 'Doesn't seem to have done you any good.'

'Alfie Halliday!' His mother batted him around the head with the newspaper. 'I'll have you doing lines after breakfast. Don't be rude! And don't talk with your mouth full.'

'Hey, lighten up, dude!' said G-Mamma from the counter, where she was loading her dish with a hillock of Cheerios. It took Janey a moment or two to realise that her godmother was talking to Mrs Halliday. G- Mamma stood between the doors of the double fridge, bouncing them off either hip in time to her new rap as she emptied a lake of milk on to her cereal. 'Yeah. Lighten up. Check it out:

Lighten up, dude It's only food
And you're the fool To think it's rude
Lighten up, Ma He's come so far And it's only gross
If the food's been chewed . . .'

144

'That's enough, Rosie,' barked Mrs Halliday suddenly. 'Behave yourself, and act your age, or there'll be lines for you too. "I will not rap at mealtimes." One hundred times!'

Janey was a bit taken aback at the headmistress's sharp response. She looked over at Bert, whose narrowed eyes were flicking between G-Mamma and Mrs Halliday as if he was watching a tennis match. 'Sorry, Bert, I think we're all a bit tetchy. Not much sleep with worrying about the sheep.'

G-Mamma leaped instantly into action again, scooting around the tiles yelling, "Not much sleep cos of all those sheep! Ye-erp . . . ye-erp, ye-erp. No shuteye when your sheep must fly! Ye-erp . . . ye- erp, ye-erp,' as Mrs Halliday scraped back her chair and wagged a finger at her, Alfie droned, 'Oh, not again,' and started pelting G-Mamma with globules of wet cornflakes, and Chloe shuffled around the table, muttering to herself.

'Sorry, what a mess,' Janey heard her say. 'Oh, sorry, Alfie, don't you like your cereal? I could make something else. Sorry.'

What on earth was wrong with everyone?

Bert had clearly had enough. He waited until one of G-Mamma's body-popping circuits had taken her safely off his route, rammed his hat on his head and scarpered for the back door. 'Gotta go. Got some proper sheep arriving,' he said to nobody in particular.

Janey grabbed a piece of bread from the basket in the middle of the table and followed him. 'Bert, wait for me!' She caught him up as he strode off towards the high gates with DUBBO SEVEN in spiky gold lettering silhouetted against the skyline. 'You ran off pretty quickly.'

'Not really my kind of people,' said Bert slowly. 'That mad woman, wotsername . . . Rose? Rosie? She's a bit . . . well, scary, if you ask me. I've never met a woman who could eat all my rock cakes at one sitting.'

Janey thought she heard a tiny tinge of grudging admiration in his tone as she scurried to keep up with his long gait. 'She's not that bad usually. None of them are. G . . . I mean, Rosie doesn't normally rap *all* the time, and Alfie isn't usually as mean as that, not deliberately anyway, and Mrs Halliday – well, she is a headmistress, but she's not usually all school-marmy like this morning *outside* of school.'

'Right,' said Bert. 'So they saved it all up for me, eh? Ha. I have to tell you, Janey, life was a lot quieter before they all turned up. Before your father turned up offering to buy me out, now I think about it. And I'm not sure now whether I should just have stuck with me good old curly-haired sheep and less money. Yeah, mate. Less money, less hassle, fewer weirdos.'

'I think maybe it's the heat,' said Janey apologetically. 'They're just not quite themselves at the moment.' She stopped suddenly. 'Neither's my dad really. I could say the same thing about him. In fact, I *did* say the same thing about him.'

It was true. Everyone, her dad included, was acting in a very extreme sort of fashion. It wasn't that they weren't being themselves exactly. Quite the opposite – they were even *more* like themselves than they usually were. She couldn't comment on Chloe, naturally, although sometimes she wanted to shake her to stop her being quite so wet. Why had their father taken Chloe when they were separated at birth? Perhaps it was a sign of Janey's strength right from the moment they were born – that she could survive without his constant care.

'Well, I've got some normal sheep arriving in a bit,' said Bert with some relief. 'I'll be back on familiar ground then. Talking of which,' he said, turning to her with a broad grin that creased his leathery face and exposed a fine gold canine tooth, 'you're on Aussie turf now, girl. How do you feel about throwing a boomerang?'

Janey grinned. 'My dad sent me one! I haven't tried it though.'

'You come with me.'

In the paddock nearest the gate, the two of them spent a happy half-hour, Bert demonstrating how to sweep the boomerang through the air so that it spun, with its strange *floop-floop* sound, right around the field to land back near his feet. Correcting Janey's stance and her elbow, he helped her to figure out how to make it feel exactly right, so that she let out a holler of joy just as the truck containing the new sheep trundled through the Dubbo Seven gates. 'I did it! Right back to my hand! That's two things I'm good at now – blowing bubblegum bubbles, and throwing boomerangs.'

'Well done, Janey,' said Bert with his slow smile. 'We'll make an Aussie of you yet. Want to help me unload?'

Tucking the boomerang into the back of her jeans, Janey readily obliged, slapping woolly backs and clapping her hands at the sheep to funnel them into the field. After a few moments Trouble began to help them, bouncing around behind the sheep in the truck to force them down the ramp and through the gate. He still looked like Trouble the Spycat, with his golden go-faster stripes down his sides and a great floppy Elvis quiff waggling madly as he jumped up and down, but even *he* was acting strangely. He loved her father, so why he had nearly chopped his hand off at the wrist was something of mystery. And why was he so attached to that handkerchief?

'That's the lot then.' Bert slammed the gate shut and drove a peg through the iron loop to keep it closed. 'Thanks, Janey. You and your . . . your cat were a lot of help.'

Janey scratched the back of a nearby sheep. 'They're nice. Maddy will be much more at home with this lot,' she said. 'I'll go and get her.'

Maddy was probably camped out behind the Spylab, close but not too close to the strange-looking, odd-smelling (too clean, Janey decided) sheep she'd helped create. With Trouble trotting eagerly at her side, Janey walked away from the gates, back past the house. Near the veranda, she paused: it had been fun spending some the morning with Bert, but her friends and family, even a brand-new sister, were right here. It was time she enjoyed their company instead. Besides, there were a few things she needed to find out.

When she walked through the back door, however, Janey stopped short. The scene before her looked like a photograph, with Alfie and Chloe on one side of the table, slumped at the shoulders and staring blankly into space, and Mrs Halliday and G-Mamma in almost identical positions opposite them, except that G-Mamma had a long trail of jam dripping from one side of her mouth. Several flies were buzzing fretfully around it; even when one landed on her lip, G-Mamma didn't twitch to move it away. They looked like shop dummies or something . . .

'G-Mamma!' shouted Janey suddenly. 'There are flies all over your face!'

At the sound of her voice, all four suddenly sprang to attention. 'Dratted flies!' yelled G-Mamma, swatting at her face with both hands with such ferocity that her cheeks were scarlet in seconds. 'Shoo, fly, don't bother me!'

'Good morning, Janey! Do join us,' said Mrs Halliday brightly, clapping her hands in a commanding fashion. 'Sit!'

'OK,' said Janey slowly as Alfie and Chloe shuffled apart and pulled out a chair for her sit on. 'Are you all right? You were all in a trance or something.'

'Thinking,' said Alfie, nodding seriously. 'It's hard when you're as thick as G-Mamma and as pathetic as Chloe.'

'Sorry, Janey,' said Chloe, starting to cry gently at what Alfie had just said. 'You didn't have much breakfast. Shall I make you some more?'

Janey shook her head. 'I'm fine, thanks. Alfie, please don't be mean to Chloe. Is . . . is everyone all right? G-Mamma, you were sort of weak last night. Are you OK now?'

'Fine and dandy, Mandy. I mean, Jandy. Janey. Zany Janey. The main Jane with a pain . . .' G-Mamma stopped short at a warning glance from Mrs Halliday.

They were all looking at Janey expectantly, so she pressed on. 'Do you think Dad's OK?'

'Fine!' they chorused.

Janey twitched uncomfortably. It was like they were all hiding something from her. 'You would tell me if something was wrong, wouldn't you? Mrs H, you weren't very happy about the sheep thing.'

'The sheep thing is really rather breathtakingly brilliant, now I come to think about it,' said Mrs Halliday decisively. It was rather an abrupt turnaround from the previous night, but Janey supposed that, in a way, she had to agree. The super-SPI pointed at Janey's plate. 'Eat your breakfast, Janey, if you don't want detention.'

'Detention?' What was wrong with Mrs Halliday? She was never this strict outside of school. In fact, come to think of it, she wasn't this strict *inside* school. Janey had to get her – in fact, all of them – to focus. 'What about that message? The one you got from Dad saying I was in trouble. Do you think I *am* in trouble?'

Alfie shook his head with a scathing expression. 'What kind of trouble could you be in? We're all here, you're with your dad, you've got a new sister. So a couple of your hairs have been used in an experiment. Big hairy deal. That message was probably just a joke. Or maybe, Miss Brilliant Blonde, you didn't interpret it properly.'

'But . . . we all saw it. G-Mamma worked it out, and your mum, and we all thought it meant the same thing. Didn't we?'

G-Mamma stared at the ceiling, scratching her chin. 'Hm, we-ell. What was it again? A bird, some legs, inside the puddy tummy. It probably just meant "Don't forget to feed the cat."'

'With human legs?' Janey looked around anxiously. She was always the best at interpreting her father's clues, so she was sure she couldn't be too far off the mark, but now the team were all staring at her, heads cocked one side as though she were an interesting specimen in a cage and not for one moment someone who ought to be believed. 'What would the legs mean?'

'Easy,' said G-Mamma with a click of her fingers. 'Walk. They mean, "walk". Get off your bony be-hind and feed the cat.'

'I really don't think that's it,' she said, shifting uneasily on her chair. Alfie and Chloe suddenly seemed incredibly close to her, and she was finding it all a bit sweaty.

'Don't you?' said Mrs Halliday. 'Oh well.'

Oh well? What did that mean? Janey knew the tone – it was the teacher or parent tone that said: "what do you know? You're just a kid!" Mrs Halliday never treated her like that.

No. There was something very odd happening: something very peculiar in the way Alfie and Chloe were closing on her, each now pressing against an arm; something really strange about how G-Mamma was sticking out her tummy to shove the kitchen table across the floor, over the tiles towards Janey so that the table edge was digging into her own stomach, trapping her in a little chair cage between her sister, her best friend and the furniture; something very sinister in the way Mrs Halliday was shoving back her chair, shaking her head with a look of disappointment as she towered over Janey's head, her sharp teeth looking over Janey's forehead like a shark that was about to decapitate her. 'Do join us, Janey. Sit!' said the headmistress for the third time in a very short space of time . . .

And suddenly everything fell in to place. The hair missing from her bedroom. Alfie's stolen handkerchief. G-Mamma seeming to be in two places at once and having needles stuck in her. Even Mrs Halliday's radical about-face in her opinions since last night. All joined together with her father's explanation of the sheep-clones: 'I can make a reasonable copy with a very limited amount of DNA.'

Janey closed her eyes in horror, and as she did so she pictured yet another image – the little patch of Chloe sick on the bottom of the SPIral staircase. 'Oh no. No, no, no. You're not spies at all, are you? You're not my friends. You're not . . . oh yuck . . . Chloe, you're not really my sister! You're – you're me! That's why you disappeared that night in the Spylab. You . . . dissolved trying to get to the SPIral, like the sheep do in the field. Yuck! Double yuck! You're all clones. My dad's made clones of you all!'

'Well, duh,' said the Alfie copy. 'Took you long enough, Blonde.'

'Get away from me!' Janey ducked to avoid his outstretched arms. 'Where's the real Alfie? What have you done with everybody? Why did my dad DO this?' It was Janey's last thought as the chair legs snapped beneath her, and four clammy pairs of hands, so familiar and yet completely unknown, reached out to grab her.

Chapter 18 Family and friends

L eave her alone!' cried a voice from the doorway.
Janey dodged the damp, sticky hands that were about to close on each limb and swivelled around, hoping desperately that it was Bert in the doorway. The tall figure, a black silhouette against the glaring sunshine, stepped into the room.

'Not yet,' said Abe. 'We still need Janey to have all her spy memories, for now.'

'Are you even my . . . my dad?' Janey lay on the floor staring fearfully at the man she had thought was her father, but who seemed suddenly to be something quite different.

He held out his hands, twinkling with Abe's trademark smile. 'What do you think?'

The Alfie-clone went to help Janey sit up but she shrugged off the hand in disgust and got to her feet. 'You can't be. My dad would never trick me like that, or make copies of his friends.'

'I'm not sure that's strictly true, young Janey,' said Abe, helping himself to an apple from the kitchen table. 'Didn't your father pretend for most of your life that he was dead? That's a pretty big trick, if you ask me. And a mean one too. As for making copies of his friends, don't you remember the reason Maisie Halliday has those terrible teeth? He turned her into a snow-woman! She was never quite the same again. Your father is no saint, believe me.'

Janey seethed, her heart thumping wildly beneath her T-shirt. What he said was true, and that was partly what made her angry. The real cause of her rage, though, was that this person who looked just like her father, and acted more-or- less like her dad, was evidently an imposter. She'd been tricked. Again. 'He had his reasons,' she said through clenched teeth. 'And you've just proved to me that you're not my father by being so cold and uncaring. I should have known that too. You've been really weird since the moment I arrived.'

'Well, yes, that was a bit of a surprise,' admitted the fake Abe. 'Arriving on your own like that. I'd planned on sending another Chloe to persuade you to come back with her, after dropping off my little clues about working on twins and being here at Dubbo Seven, but you took matters into your own hands. Initiative, Blonde. One of your better qualities.'

'But we dusted the box for fingerprints, and they were definitely Abe's, so you're . . . another clone?'

'Correct,' said the Abe replica. 'A copy. A facsimile.'

'But that means . . .' Janey thought as rapidly as she could as five flat, lifeless sets of eyes focused on her. 'That means someone made you in the first place!'

'Right again,' he said, a slow smile spreading across his face as he witnessed Janey's expression of horror and loathing. 'And who do you think would have the power and the genius to do that?'

'No,' said Janey, swallowing hard. 'Only my dad could do that, and he wouldn't be that horrible.'

At this the Abe copy spun around, slamming his fist against the table. 'Your father is not the only one who could do that! He can't do what we've done here. For once we're a step ahead of him – several steps, in fact! So don't go on about your precious father as if he's the only genius around. Think, Blonde. Who else?'

And as she saw the mocking victory in the clones" expressions, Janey's heart sank. 'Not . . . not Copernicus. He's been kept out of harm's way!'

'Yes,' hissed the Abe copy. 'In a deep freeze far away – isn't that right, Blonde? Wrong! As soon as he became involved in the power-struggle with your father, Copernicus injected himself with tracer cells. His aides have been able to track him down and thaw him out. And unfortunately for you, your father hadn't been too careful about the freezing process. He left his own DNA tracks all over Copernicus. And so –' He turned in the doorway, hands aloft, looking so like Abraham Rownigan, Janey's father, that she felt a familiar buzz across the bridge of her nose. Tears were on the way – 'here I am.'

Five sets of eyes were still fixed on Janey. She knew that she needed to think quickly, make a plan and find her friends, but somehow her brain felt foggy and soup-like. It was all too much to take in, and she knew that she wasn't

156

at the very bottom of it even now. 'You,' she said hoarsely, pointing at Chloe. 'You're not even real. I don't have a twin at all, do I?'

Her own grey eyes returned her gaze sorrowfully. 'Sorry, Janey. No you don't. I was made from that hair you stuck on your SPI-buys box.'

Janey felt sick. She'd believed it all, and dreamed of the happy life they would all share here at Dubbo Seven. Even that had been a sign – the logo that branded the sheep farm from above the gates: Dubbo in a spiky golden crown over the number seven, exactly as the Sun King, Copernicus, had marked his presence at Sunny Jim's Swims. She should have seen it, should have trusted the instincts that were telling her something was not right; that her father, the set- up here, his strange sheep and the way he treated everybody – it just wasn't right.

And suddenly another emotion started to bubble under the fear that swirled through her chest.

Relief.

The whole story about her father giving up Solomon's Polifications Investigations had been simply a ploy – a way to get her over to Australia and the Spylab. Her father had no intention of giving up SPI, and Janey – Jane Blonde – was not giving up either.

'Time you stopped playing, Blonde,' drawled the Alfie copy.

'You shut up!' Janey could stand the real Alfie being a bit snarky – it was just his manner, and his way of being funny – but the Alfie-clone was a nastier version. G-Mamma was a crazier, more cartoonish version of herself, and Mrs Halliday much stricter and more headmistress-like. The SPI-clone had taken each of their characteristics and made them into a caricature of themselves, through the DNA from Alfie's handkerchief, the cell-sucking syringe that had been sunk into G-Mamma's behind and whatever method of DNA-extraction they'd used on Mrs Halliday.

'Where are they?' Janey drew herself up to her full height to make herself look as powerful as possible. It wasn't easy in cut-offs and a top with a puppy on it. If only she was in her SPIsuit. 'Where are the real Alfie and his mum, and G-Mamma? If you've hurt them, I'll . . .'

'You'll do nothing,' spat the Abe-clone, grabbing her arm roughly. 'You're helpless against us, Brown. These may be weak clones, made from the DNA we were able to steal, but now I've got the original bodies I can make as many copies as I like. We just need to add a couple more to the collection so as not to cause any suspicion anywhere, and then the SPI-clone will be put to far better use than sending out sheep. If we so choose, there will be whole armies of spies, cloned to the Sun King's specifications, ready to fight your father if he ever dares to come out of the shadows and confront us.'

'He will!' screamed Janey. 'You know he will!'

The Abe-clone drew in a deep breath. 'I doubt it,' he said at length, 'because he'll never know. Who's going to tell him? You? I don't think so. You won't be able to remember a thing. You'll barely be functioning, in fact. Just a steady supply of DNA from a super-SPI gene pool.'

Janey racked her brains trying to think, her eyes darting this way and that as she looked frantically for a way out. She had to stay alive – and keep her spy mentality – to be able to fight them off. She would have to stall for time.

'So the . . . the long-haired sheep, and the farm and all that. You don't need any of it? You just used Bert!' Groping behind her on the table, she managed to pick up a jammy butter-knife and stick it in her back pocket.

The clone team grouped themselves around the Abe-clone; it was a formidable if slightly grey and greasy group of spies that faced her. Fake-Abe shook his head. 'On the contrary. The plans that Copernicus has are – shall we say – expensive. And his government funding seems to have run out!' The gaggle of clones laughed moronically. 'These scientific breakthroughs will provide money. Lots of it, and quickly. This is just the beginning. Imagine what riches Copernicus will have when he dominates the world's clothing industry with his super-sheep, the milk industry with his super- cows . . .'

'He's mad.' Janey got a careful grip on the knife in her pocket.

'The world's his oyster, you mean,' said the Abe-clone. 'And it doesn't stop there!'

Janey wasn't sure what he meant by that, but she was sufficiently sure that the Abe-clone needed whatever

159

information he thought she had to enable her to keep playing for time. Whatever insane plans for world domination Copernicus might be harbouring, he would not triumph. She could stop this, somehow. Dropping down low, she whipped the knife around in front of her. 'Stay back!' she cried, pointing the strawberry-jammy knife-tip at each of the clones in turn.

Abe smiled slowly. 'Kill them, Janey. I dare you. Kill them all, if you can, with that blunt piece of metal.'

'Yeah,' said the Alfie-clone with a nasty smile. 'A sticky, buttery knife. What are you going to do, kill us *scone* dead?'

The clones threw their heads back and howled with laughter, except Abe who simply looked pitifully at Janey. 'Do your worst, Blonde. There will always be more.'

At that, he let out a slow whistle, and to Janey's horror another set of clones instantly appeared at the back door. 'Now, there's just one little piece of information I need out of you. Do sit down.'

Janey looked around. There was no way out – the two G-Mamma clones had moved around to block the kitchen door, and there were cloned spies all around her, looking so horribly like her friends, even like herself, but filled with poison in a way that her team would never be. She still wasn't about to give in, however.

'You won't get anything out of me,' she said, steadying her voice as much as she could. 'I'm a true Spylet. I won't tell.'

The Abe-clone sighed. 'All right, Janey. If you insist on doing this the hard way, so be it. Chloe One,' he said to the Janey-clone behind him. 'Get her, now.' Janey jumped, ready to tackle her mirror image, but to her surprise the clone, Chloe One, turned and walked out of the house. What was she going to do to her? Perhaps she was getting some instrument of torture to make her talk. Janey paced nervously, circling the kitchen table and making hopeless jabs at the clones with her silly knife.

Abe checked his watch. 'You others had better hide.'

The clones nodded robotically and melted away through the doorways, out on to the veranda, into the large walk-in pantry, or along the hall to the bedrooms. Before too long there were just the Abe-clone and Janey left in the room, and he looked up at her with a strange expression, almost of amusement. 'You will talk, my dear,' he said eventually. 'If you want to stop us from getting the full set of your family's super-SPI.' And he started to laugh, just as Janey heard Chloe's thin voice outside.

'Close your eyes and count to ten, and then go inside. I'm going the other way.'

'This had better be worth it, Janey,' said a familiar voice, and Janey's heart sank.

The full set. All the genes Copernicus needed to make a spy super-race, cloning as many as he could possibly need to run his empire. She now knew what he'd meant, and who Chloe had to "get'. It wasn't Janey. It was the one

161

person in the whole wide world she cared about as much as her father, and that was why she would talk.

'Ten!' she heard the voice say outside, and tears filled her eyes as Jean Brown, tired and confused, stepped off the veranda and in through the back door.

Chapter 19 A dressing down

Janey's mum swivelled on her thick, sensible heels, looking from Janey to the Abe-clone and back again.

'Abe!' she said, trying to sound casual but hardly able to disguise the pleased note in her voice. She hadn't laid eyes on him since they had established Abe 'n' Jean's Clean Machines and shared a few spag bols and a bit of kite-flying, and even though she professed to be quite fine about it, Janey knew that her mother thought about him often. What Jane didn't know was that she was actually thinking about her own husband, Janey's father.

Janey dropped her knife on the table and ran over to her mum. She threw both arms around her middle and squeezed as hard as she could. 'Well, you're obviously feeling better!' Jean laughed, holding Janey at arm's length so she could see her better. 'That cottage in Wales obviously did you the world of good. Thanks for organizing that for us, Abe. It was such a nice surprise finding Janey there waiting for me, even if she was looking a bit peaky and had to go to bed so early each evening.'

'But Mum, it wasn't . . .'

'My pleasure,' interrupted the Abe-clone, raising an eyebrow at Janey. It was enough to silence her, and in the pause that followed she processed what her mum had just said. The little getaway that her mum had disappeared on had obviously been set up by Copernicus. He'd even sent a Janey-clone to keep her mum company, so that she wouldn't start to question why her daughter was away so long – not that Janey could be sure how long it had been, since day blended into night and time had become caught up in a great confusing loop around the world.

She loosened her grip on her mum a little. 'So, are you OK?' There was always the chance that the Jean Brown figure before her was also a clone, so she looked right into her mother's face to check that her eyes were alight with her mum's soul and grasped her hands carefully. They were warm and dry, exempt from the cold dampness that Janey now realised had characterized the hands of the other clones.

'Ye-es,' said Jean, scanning Janey's face. 'Still OK, from when you just left me outside. And Abe – thank you again. I never expected that we'd be able to come and see you in Australia. That is where we are, isn't it? I must have severe jet lag or something. The journey seems . . . well, I don't remember it at all. Just Janey saying the taxi was here and the tickets had arrived.'

'Yes, you're in Australia, at my sheep farm – Dubbo Seven.' The Abe-clone kissed Jean's hand formally, and Janey had to fight off the temptation to smack her mum's wrist away from those slimy, unnatural lips. 'Welcome. I'm sure you'll love it here. I hope you can stay . . . a very long time.'

'Well, it's only the Easter holidays,' said Jean, unconsciously wiping the back of her hand against her thick woollen skirt. The lips must have felt as odd as they now looked to Janey. 'Just a fortnight – I'd have to ask permission from the headmistress at Janey's school—'

'Granted!' cried one of the headmistress clones, stepping smartly out from the hallway.

'Oh! You're here!' Jean looked confused. 'And Alfie too. That's . . . wonderful. Company for Janey.'

'Me too!' A large shimmering figure bobbed out from the pantry, tell-tale eating tracks running like snail-slime down her vermilion top. 'Remember me? Your neighbour.'

Jean's semi-pleased expression quickly disappeared. 'What are you doing here?'

'I like that! Not everybody hates me, you know, Jeany Beany Quite the Meany. Maisie is my *friend*! Yes, and so is Abe, and Alfie and –' G-Mamma flapped a hand at Janey – '. . . your, um, lovely daughter-thing. Janey. Zany Janey. Jane the pain who should be slain. Ha! Just kidding.'

G-Mamma had just confirmed that she was every bit as mad as Jean had suspected and Janey's mum was starting to look rather uncomfortable as she looked at Abe, hoping for some explanation. The only words he offered, however, brought a chill to Janey's spine. 'It's been a long journey, Jean. Look, Janey and I were just in the middle of a very interesting discussion. Why don't you let Maisie

165

take you to your . . . room. And then Janey can join you just as soon as we've finished here.'

'All right,' said Jean shortly. 'But don't be long.' As soon as the door closed behind the Alfie and G-Mamma clones, who also left the room, Abe-clone turned to Janey. 'Start talking, and quickly, and no harm will come to her.'

'You need her genes!' said Janey quickly. 'You can't harm her.'

'I can manage with the genes I've got.' He leaned in close. 'Have no fear of that. If you tell me what I want to know, I'll send her back without a scratch. I'll even supply her with a Chloe, so she never even knows what's happened. It's up to you, Brown.'

'The name's Blonde. Jane Blonde,' said Janey irritably, even though right now she felt like plain Janey Brown, a schoolgirl in jeans, who had to do everything in her power to save her mother. She stared at the table.

'Tick tock,' said the Abe-clone in a menacing whisper.

'All right! What do you want to know?'

The Abe-clone's eyes gleamed momentarily. 'The first time you arrived here, you didn't come in the SPIral. How did you get here?'

Janey stared at him. 'The . . . you didn't send. . .?'

STOP! Janey screamed at herself. He hadn't sent the ESPIdrills. The fake Abe had been planning that Chloe would bring Janey to him, which could only mean that the eSPIdrills really were sent by her father. He had wanted her to come to him . . .

'Your father supplied your transport method – that much I know. He thinks he's got some advantage over us because of that. Some clue to what he's been working on. Obviously he's not going to tell us himself, so his dear little girl will have to spills the beans.'

'Airline tickets,' said Janey, folding her arms. 'That's what he sent me. I came by plane and then helicopter, like I told Bert when I first arrived.'

'Don't underestimate me, Brown.'

'It's true.'

With an exaggerated sigh, Fake-Abe stood up. 'Well, if you're not prepared to tell me, I'll just have to deal with your mother . . .'

'No! All right, I'll tell you!' Janey's throat closed up with fear. Her mum was totally innocent in all of this. She'd have no idea what was happening, and it was so unfair to her. She had to protect her! She had to confess. 'It was these shoes – eSPIdrills. Earth- moving SPI drills.'

There was a gasp. 'You came through the centre of the earth?' Fake-Abe stared at her for a long moment, then his eyes moved off her to stare into the corners of the kitchen with that same strange look of calculation she had noticed before.

'I've told you now,' said Janey. 'Let Mum go free.'

Abe-clone pondered for a moment, then nodded.

'She's no loss. I can extract Jean's genes without her even being aware of it and send her back home where she will continue to be no trouble at all. You, on the other hand . . .'

Janey tried to back away as the tall figure stood and gripped her by the shoulders. 'What? What do you mean?'

'I could do with a little army of Jane Blondes,' he said softly, spinning her towards the hall door. 'What am I saying? Of course, I mean a big army. I've only made Chloes from Janey Brown genes so far, and a few Blonde experiments with DNA we've garnered from your SPIsuit and so on.'

'That's why Chloe washed it!' Janey could have kicked herself. 'And why you wouldn't let me de-Wow.'

'And now I won't let you leave at all. We'll have the original Jane Blonde. Stronger copies, you'll recall. I'll keep you here, extract your genes and keep you completely safe, and turn a Jane Blonde battalion against her own father's organisation. Superb.'

'You'll do that? Don't you mean Copernicus?' cried Janey, trying to wriggle out of the ever-increasing pressure of the Abe-clone's long fingers.

He gave a shrug of the shoulders as he pushed her towards Chloe's bedroom. 'We are so close, my dear – he will definitely approve. Come. It's time for a little more hair-brushing.'

Bewildered, whipping her head left and right as she looked for her mother, Janey found herself pushed through

Chloe's door, passed from hand to clammy hand along the row of G-Mamma-clone, Halo-clone, Alfie-clone, and finally her very own clone, Chloe, who pushed her bottom lip out as her eyes filled with tears. 'Sorry, Janey. But you won't feel anything.'

'No!' she screamed as the five clones shoved her on to the stool before the dressing table and Chloe picked up the hairbrush. Suddenly memories flooded back to her: the sick and woozy feeling that had come over her there before, the horrible voice like her father's pronouncing that he despised her, Trouble's sabre- claw slicing through her leg . . .

'This dressing table –' she cried, ducking to evade the hairbrush for as long as she could, 'it's . . . haunted or something!'

The Alfie-clone rolled his eyes. 'Haunted? Is that the best you can do? It's not even a dressing table, Brainless. It's a DeSpies-U.'

Janey gasped. Not "despise" – it wasn't her father telling her he hated her. It was even worse than that! A DeSpies-U! She would be de-spied, stripped of all her spying past and training and knowledge, left like a shell to be drained of DNA, to be used whenever it was needed to create a SWAT team, or a battle battalion, or a complete hideous army of killer Blondes. The hairbrush was on her head. A chant was starting up: Jane Blonde, DeSpies-U. Jane Blonde, Despise-U. She had to think, to get out . . .

And following one of the strongest instincts that she had – one that had existed within her long before she'd ever known she was a spy – Janey allowed the floodgates behind her eyes to open and burst into noisy sobs. 'Stop!' she wailed. 'At least let me say goodbye to my mum. You pro-ho-mised!'

Chloe's hand halted in mid-air. The chanting subsided, and Janey found herself staring into the cold eyes of Fake-Abe in the dressing-table mirror. How could she ever have believed that this was her father? He belonged in Madame Tussaud's, in the section for hideous murderers. 'Honour among spies,' he said suddenly, with a vicious twist of his lips. 'I don't remember your father having much of that, Blonde. But you're right. I did promise. And I, at least, know how to do the right thing. You lot,' he said to the clone team, 'back away. I'll go and get the Brown woman. We'll be back on track in just a couple of minutes.'

Janey watched slyly, being careful to sob from time to time as the two Halliday-clones moved off to either side of the bed and pretended to be straightening the duvet and the G-Mamma-clone busied herself with the curtains. Chloe slid under the bed, and was completely out of sight by the time Jean was led into the room by the man she thought was Abe Rownigan.

'Hello, sweetheart,' she said. Janey patted the seat next to her and her mother sat down and hugged her. 'Abe tells me you're a bit tired and going to have a lie-down? I can't say I'm surprised, what with you disappearing to bed at sunset each night in Wales.'

Janey stared into her mother's eyes, and now the tears flowed for real. Unless her plan worked (and there was no saying that it would) this could be the very last time she would see her mum. Jean would go back home, assuming the Abe-clone kept his other promise and allowed her to live, and would never know that the Janey who was sleeping in the next room and eating at the same table was not her Janey at all, but just a sad, thin, heartless copy. She held her mother as tightly as she could. 'Love you, Mum,' she whispered.

'I love you too,' said her mum, perplexed. 'What's the matter?'

Janey shook herself and smiled at her mother. 'Nothing. Hey, do you remember what we used to do when I was really, really little?'

'What, sweetheart?'

'This,' said Janey and, picking up the hairbrush, she stood up and ran the bristles across her mother's smooth brown hair. Fake-Abe looked puzzled, and Janey smiled at him brightly. 'It's a mother–daughter thing,' she said, brushing harder, then harder still as she saw her mother's eyes closing, heard the faint whisper from the dressing table starting up, getting louder, and louder as Jean Brown's head began to nod against her chest . . .

And just as Jean began to snore and the woozy feeling was beginning to consume Janey, she jumped back out of

171

range of the creeping, insidious sounds and, remembering that it was only Trouble's sharp claw in her thigh that had made her come to, she dropped the hairbrush on to her mum's crown with a loud crack.

Jean sat up with a start and scanned the mirror quickly. 'Well, well,' she said with narrowed eyes, hazel and glowing as a cat's. 'What have we here?'

Chapter 20 Jean genie

J aney looked her mother up and down quickly. Her mum hadn't been Wowed, so she still looked like ordinary, sensible Jean Brown, but as Janey had hoped would happen, the DeSpies-U had worked in reverse on someone who had already been de-spied in the past . . .

Gina Bellarina was back in force.

The immediate problem was that Gina Bellarina recognized all of the spies around her as her friends and allies. Janey had to put her straight quickly. Brandishing the hairbrush, Janey spun around to face the Abe-clone. 'These are enemies, Mum. They're all clones. There's one of me under the bed, and that Abe one there–' she poked the brush in his direction – 'is working for Copernicus. I don't know where the real spies are, but we have to help them. Quick!'

'He *cloned* you? Are you saying that that was a feeble Janey clone in Wales? How corrupt. Leave this to me, Blonde.' Gina Bellarina allowed herself a small, steely smile and clapped her hands briskly. 'I'm going to enjoy this. You go and find the others – let's hope we're still in time. Yaaaaa!'

With a blood-curdling war cry, Gina whisked into action. The Halliday-clones headed straight for her so she stood on the dressing-table stool and bounced neatly over their heads, kicking each of them at chest height at such an angle that they clanged heads in the middle and collapsed in a heap on the carpet. Gina landed on the bed, sprang up and somersaulted, then immediately launched herself over the Abe-clone to the curtain pole, hanging from it like a long-limbed spider as she twirled her legs around and around, capturing G-Mamma in a curtain cocoon. The G-Mamma-clone blundered around, mummified and rapping like a broken record, as Gina Bellarina gripped the curtain pole firmly in both hands, swung back through the open window in a high arc then swept down and back inside, both feet in front of her.

'Go, Blonde!' she called out to an admiring Janey, as she caught Fake-Abe full under the chin in a double-barrelled foot assault that left him sprawled across the bed groaning. The Alfie-clone had managed to get up again – Janey just had time to see her mother crack her fingers in readiness for a renewed attack before she pelted down the hallway towards the front door.

On her way past, Janey flung every door open and hollered for her spy team, dropping on to her knees to check under the beds. There was nothing to see apart from the odd patch of clear gloop – dissolved clones, she now knew. That was why they'd faded each night, feigning food poisoning in order to avoid disappearing before her very eyes. She moved on as quickly as she could, but felt severely hampered by her jeans and ordinary trainers. Running through the front door, she leaped on the quadbike that Chloe had driven, tried to remember what she could about driving and turned the key in the ignition.

To her joy, it burst into life and soon she was careering between gates and trees and launching herself off banks of packed earth to sail, whooping merrily, across the Dubbo Seven Pastures. It only took a couple of minutes to get where she wanted, and she knew that what she would achieve would more than make up for the journey time. Slithering off the seat, Janey hauled the four metal water troughs into position and turned the temporary Wower on full.

The blissful feeling of power was instantaneous, and Janey threw her head back in relief as the transformation to Jane Blonde took place. It was unusual to be able to see blue sky above her head through the sparkling moisture, and she gasped at the fabulous rainbow arcing in a fairy-tale roof over the Wower. Multicoloured droplets shimmered all around her, caught in the prism of light. The effect was startlingly beautiful, and Janey almost laughed aloud as the robotic hand styled her hair. Through one of the gaps between the troughs, she suddenly noticed two pairs of eyes, one above the other. Just as she was about to cry out, the top set jumped down and ran towards her, and suddenly there was Trouble, whisking around her ankles, enjoying being Wowed every bit as much as Janey. All signs of his strange caution had gone, and all at once Janey understood just what he had been through.

'Oh, Trouble! You've known all along! That's why you didn't like Abe, and why you stabbed me in the leg – to get me away from the DeSpies-U. Clever cat!'

The Wower stopped abruptly, and Jane Blonde stepped out into the sunshine. 'Trouble, go and find Gina. She might need back-up. Take Maddy with you,' she said, quickly identifying the other pair of eyes near the Wower. 'Don't let her get hurt, OK? I'm going to find the others.'

Her search of the house had revealed no sign of any of them, so now Janey dropped her head to avoid the sun's glare and scanned the horizon through her Ultra-gogs. 'Err, detect!' she said, a little unsure how to phrase what she was trying to say. 'Detect body heat.'

It was a new instruction, but evidently one that the Ultra-gogs were able to comply with. Within seconds the image in her narrow band of vision had turned black, and every now and again she could see a little glowing outline. Each body had its own little prism of light, she realised. 'OK, now I see. Zoom – through the bedroom window. Two tall, one wide, two shorter, all very still – that's all the clones who were attacking Mum. She must have tied them up.' She turned her head. 'Ah, there's Mum, checking the bedrooms. And Bert with his sheep.'

The Spy-cloned sheep were still ambling around behind the Spylab, as Janey could see by the faint glowing outlines in the nearby paddock. Fainter still – in fact, only just visible even when she peered at them really closely – were four rounded outlines nearby. She couldn't work out what they were, or even where they were, and it was not until she lifted her gaze above the top edge of her Ultra-gogs that Janey realised exactly what she was looking at. There were four very slight pools of body heat somewhere within the Spylab. With a gasp, Janey took to her Fleet-feet.

It was the obvious place to keep them – right where they could be trundled under the Spy-clone in moments. Janey pounded across acres of grass at a staggering speed, hurdling fences as though they were only ankle height. Only a few minutes later she was skirting the silky sheep, wondering how Bert would feel if he knew the truth about their freakish origins. No wonder they all bleated the same note! She arrived at the Spylab door, panting only slightly, and ordered her Ultra-gogs to "detect" again.

Her eyes were instantly drawn to the wheeled cabinets along the back wall of the laboratory. Somewhere behind them were four sources of body heat. Janey sprinted over and pulled one of the cabinets out. It was the one Maddy had been trapped in before she was suctioned against the Spy-clone; Janey could still see little tufts of her long curly, wool wafting around the bottom like furry mice. Hurriedly she yanked the next one out from the line. Empty. So was the next one, and the next. It was hopeless. She ran right along the wall, frantically pulling out cabinets, but not a trace of a spy did she find.

'Detect!' she shouted again at the Ultra-gogs. There they were again – four distinct body shapes, although she couldn't work out who anybody was or why there were four. She could see them a little more clearly now, and the truth suddenly dawned on her. Dropping down on all fours, she shuffled under the workbench to the storage cabinets, and to her delight the images in her Ultra-gogs glowed more brightly. 'Thank goodness they're still alive,' she said under her breath.

She reached the wall behind the cabinets. It looked smooth and solid at first, but on closer inspection Janey discovered a tiny button – a Dubbo Seven logo – right under the back edge of the worktop, so small that it could easily be mistaken for a tiny rivet. Without the Ultra-gogs, she would probably never have seen it.

She held her breath and touched a finger to it. 'Hey, presto!'

The wall slid away, right and left, like the fireplace tunnel back in G-Mamma's Spylab, only horizontally. The first thing Janey saw was a bright red roller skate poking out from a shimmering lilac SPIsuit. 'G-Mamma!' Janey wobbled the foot anxiously, and to her relief her godmother's head appeared over the mound of her body like the sun rising in the east. 'Sugar,' mumbled G-Mamma through cracked,

un-glossed lips. 'Sugar now, Blonde, and that's an order!'

'Well, you're obviously all right,' said Janey with relief. 'You haven't been de-spied.. I need to help the others now.'

G-Mamma fixed Janey briefly with her wide, slightly glazed blue eyes, then collapsed back on to the concrete floor.

'Janey, never mind the sweetie monster – get us out!' It was Alfie, lying on a slender mattress and pillow but with his wrists and ankles tightly bound. The Abe- clone must have expected him to be more trouble than G-Mamma; he certainly looked a lot angrier. 'You took your time. How long have we been in here? I met myself just after we first arrived, I think. They kept sedating us so we didn't know where we were or what day it was, but nobody's been in for ages.'

'They've been too busy trying to de-spy me– and they brought my mum here. Ach!' Janey fumbled with the knots for a few moments, then stood back and directed the laser finger of her Girl-gauntlet at the ropes. Seconds later Alfie was free, scrambling along behind her.

Mrs Halliday was curled neatly in a corner. 'Janey! That is you, isn't it? I've been visited by several versions of you, some of Alfie and even one of myself. I decided to conserve my energy and not try to resist.'

'It's definitely me this time.' Janey pulled her upright and stood back to laser through her restraints. Mrs Halliday smiled wearily. 'Come on, let's grab G- Mamma and get out of here before they catch up with us.'

Janey shuffled backwards to allow them out. 'We'd better get Mum too. She's gone all Gina Bellarina at the moment – don't ask,' she added when Alfie looked at

179

her, amazed. The Hallidays reached for G-Mamma and waited while Alfie fed her a fruit chew from the pocket she directed him to. The SPI: KE brightened immediately and got on to her hands and knees. 'Well, I've had enough of that little hidey- hole, I can tell you. Yes, sirree.' Suddenly Janey stopped. 'Hang on, I forgot. There's another body, er, person here. There were definitely four shapes in the display.'

The spies weren't able to help. 'We've all been out of it, pretty much,' explained Alfie. 'We've been kept asleep except for when someone – something – brought us some food.'

Mrs Halliday nodded. 'It was always you to begin with, Janey, or so we thought, but then we realised after a few visits that it wasn't a brain-wiped Blonde, but a copy of some kind.'

'Clones.' Janey felt sick just saying it. 'Fake-Abe is an agent of Copernicus – sorry, Alfie.' Alfie had bitten his lip at the mere mention of his father. 'And he's been using that pointy thing in the middle of the lab – the Spy-clone – to make identical copies of sheep – and then of us, using our DNA.'

Just at that moment, they heard a low groan from further along the row of cupboards. The door had not slid quite far enough along, so Janey braced her feet against it and pushed. It flew back to reveal a cage in a final dank cupboard, only half the size of the cubbyholes the others had been imprisoned in. A hand, pale and missing a thumb tip, trailed through the bars on to the concrete, and Janey's throat closed as she reached out her own hand to touch it.

'It's the real Abe,' she said, her chin wobbling furiously. 'My dad.'

Clustering around the cage, the spies all looked in at Abe Rownigan. He was deathly white, his unshaven cheeks sunken and barely moving in and out with his shallow breathing. There was very little room for his long body in the cage: he was curled around with his head on his arm. His other hand clutched something to his body, so that it was mostly concealed beneath the knotty bones of his skeletal fingers.

'Dad,' Janey whispered, reaching a hand through the bars to shake his shoulder. He groaned once and shifted, but didn't awaken.

'They've put him out well and truly,' said G- Mamma, now sufficiently restored to get to her feet. 'Let's get him out of there. Stand well back.'

Janey was glad to let someone else take control. Her arms and legs were feeling peculiarly wobbly, as if all the strength – all the Blonde – had drained out of them. She watched gratefully as G-Mamma removed the linked gold belt – actually a retractable-rope device called a suSPInder – from her SPIsuit, fed it around the bars of the cage and then let it trail to several feet away. Next, she removed the chewed sweet from her mouth and stuck it to the top of the nearest bar, under the last link of the SuSPInder –. 'Laser,

Blonde,' she said to Janey, pointing to the tapered end of the belt, which lay at their feet.

Confused, but willing to do anything that would save her father, Janey directed her Girl-gauntlet at the narrow buckle and pressed. The beam of light illuminated the belt briefly, and then suddenly a tiny flame sparked up from the buckle. They all watched, fascinated and hopeful, as the flame licked along the length of the belt, and then as it reached the chewed gummy sweet and G-Mamma covered her ears delicately, there was a dull *thwump* as it detonated. The bars sheared cleanly out of their anchorage and were ejected across the floor under the workbench.

'What *is* that stuff?' said Alfie with more than a touch of envy in his voice. 'I thought it was a toffee!'

'Not for Spylets.' G-Mamma removed the sticky sweet from the top of the bars, chewed it once more for good luck and then shoved it back in her pocket. 'It's SPInamite.'

'Wow,' said Alfie, but Janey was already fighting her way through the smoke as a rasping cough erupted from the cell.

'Dad, are you OK?'

He still wasn't able to speak, but at least he was still alive. His cough was weak, and his eyes opened only once, but she took hold of his hand and felt the faint pulse in his wrist become stronger. 'It's me, Dad. Janey. Don't worry – I won't leave you.'

'What have they done to him?' G-Mamma hooked her hands under Abe's armpits and hauled him out of the cage. As he moved, the object he'd been holding came loose and clattered to the floor.

Janey picked it up. 'I think it might be what he's done to himself,' she said grimly. 'It's the remote control for the Satispy.'

'Told you it wasn't ready yet,' said Alfie, not terribly helpfully.

It wasn't ready – Alfie knew it, Janey knew it, and of course her father knew it. The Satispy had been tested only on reasonably short journeys, never on a voyage halfway around the world. Janey could barely imagine how far into space her father must have gone to get high enough to be able to zap down in Australia. The ordeal had clearly taken everything out of him – which signified one thing to Janey, and one thing only: he had been scared. Scared for Janey. Willing to risk his own life to get to her as quickly as he could. Once again her father had come to her rescue as she'd failed in her mission, and once again, there was a horrible chance that it would cost him his life.

And it was not until she heard Alfie shouting 'What the heck's that?' that Janey became aware of a great roaring gale, and she finally poked her head out from under the workbench and realised the dreadful truth.

It wasn't just going to cost her father his life.

Every single one of them was going to pay the same terrible, ultimate price. She had led them all to their deaths.

Chapter 21 Barmy army

The wind died to an eerie hush as Janey, Alfie, G-Mamma and Mrs Halliday let Abe Rownigan fall gently to the floor behind them. None of them was able to stand, partly because they were still stooped under the counter, but mainly because they were so horribly appalled at the sight that met their eyes across the floor of the Spylab that their knees buckled with fear.

The Abe-clone had been demonically busy while they had been releasing the real Abe. The lab was no longer empty. In fact, it was so full of people that Janey could no longer see the wall in any direction, as the view was obscured by bobbing heads – her own. And along with the Chloes were Alfies, G-Mammas, Mrs Hallidays and, to Janey's dismay, Gina Bellarinas, and a huge number of Jane Blondes in pale silver SPIsuits with white-blonde hair – white, she assumed, because her own blonde hair was a mix of her natural brown and Wower-created white blonde, and the hair they'd used had been a pure version of the latter. Pure Blonde. A wedge-shaped battalion of each of the spy clones – forty to fifty of each, with rather more cloned Blondes – radiated out from a central point under the sinister tip of the Spy-clone, all waiting silently for the command to attack to come from their leader.

He stood at their centre, his fake film-star grin almost splitting his face in two, and how Janey wished it would.

She wondered, for one mad moment, whether clones had all the same insides as real people. Of one thing she felt certain: – inside the chest cavity there might be an organ that beat like a heart, but there was no emotion to drive it and make it real.

'You promised to let my mum go,' said Janey eventually, her voice cutting through the silence so that she sounded rather shrill. It was impossible to know which of the Jeans, if any, was her real mother, and she very much doubted whether the Abe-clone ever intended to keep any of his promises.

The evil Abe shrugged. 'I told you she was useless to me, other than her genes. She's going to be useless to you too, now that I've de-spied her again. Bring her out, and the man too!' he shouted suddenly to a small troop of Jane Blondes standing immediately to his left.

Six Blonde-clones broke away from the main body and trotted over to the Spylab doorway. They disappeared into the sun's glare for a moment, then reappeared in the lab pulling a trailer. In it, tied hand and foot and placed back to back like human bookends, were Jean Brown and Bert. Bert's face was set in an expression of grim terror mingled with complete disbelief, while Jean just looked mightily fed up, shaking her head from time to time as if she was trying to wake herself up.

'I've had enough of this dream now!' she said to the pair of Jane Blondes on either side of her. 'This jet lag is terrible. Pretty soon I'm going to wake up, aren't I? Aren't I, whoever you are?'

Bert sighed. 'I don't know about a dream, lady,' he said shakily. 'More like some kind of nightmare. I've known all along that something wasn't right with those sheep, but this . . . this is beyond insane. I was just an ordinary farmer, you know? I didn't ask for any of this mumbo-jumbo. I wish I'd never laid eyes on ya, Rownigan! You, your people copies and your genetically modified sheep.'

Janey took a step forward. 'What are you going to do with us?' she asked as the trailer was pushed over towards them. With Mrs Halliday's help, she reached out for it and pulled the trailer to them, and G- Mamma and Alfie helped her weak, rasping father in beside Janey's mother. Janey hugged her mum quickly, noticing something angular caught between the spines of Jean and Bert. 'You've got our DNA, haven't you? Let us go!'

'You know already what I'm planning, Blonde. Don't try stalling for time. This –' and he cast his arm around the roomful of spy-clones like a conductor presenting his orchestra – 'is just the beginning. You can stay shut up back there for ever. Nobody will ever miss you – any of you. Let's face it, nobody will ever realise you're actually missing." At the snap of his fingers the door at the top of the metal stairs banged back against the wall, and half a dozen figures stepped through the door from the SPIral staircase on to the high platform above the Spylab.

'Holy granoly, that's me.' Bert whistled. He was looking directly at his own image, tall, rugged and weather-beaten, pulling his leather hat down over his eyes. Next to him was G-Mamma, dancing away to her own strange internal rhythm, and slightly behind was the Halliday family, ready for school and very un- spylike.

The last to step through the door was the unremarkable Brown family: Abe, in a pinstripe suit, ready for the office, Jean, in head-to-foot beige with an apron around her waist and a bucket and mop in one hand, and finally Janey. Janey Brown, with skinned, knobbly knees protruding out from under her school uniform. Janey Brown, lank hair tickling her collar and covering her serious grey eyes. Janey Brown. Brown by name and brown by nature. It was the cruellest trick of all, to send her back out into the world with no trace of her alter ego, of the person she had become. This clone was Brown only. She was completely devoid of Jane Blonde.

And as Janey looked around, she understood that it was hopeless. 'Lock them up!' commanded the Abe- clone, and two hundred pairs of damp-skinned arms rose up in the air, pointed towards them and started to advance. They were trapped, backed up against the counter at the back of the barn, surrounded on all sides by clones, separating into horrible look-a-like lines to attack the spy who had provided them with their own DNA, had given them life.

Alfie stepped back as dozens of Alfie-clones headed straight towards him, brandishing their Boy- battlers and sneering at him with his trademark curl of the lip. It didn't look even the tiniest bit amusing, as Alfie's often did; repeated so many times and fixed in a constant supercilious expression, it was downright sinister. Nasty. Certainly the way they were all about to pummel him with the Boy-battler gloves, and a few were doubling the gloves up in size so the acid sacs would kick into operation looked distinctly unpleasant.

'Mum, er, Mum,' said Alfie quietly, but Mrs Halliday could do nothing to help him. A troop of Agent Halos was advancing in a smart march, clapping their hands in rhythm so it sounded like a volley of gunshots, and baring and gnashing their SPI:KEd teeth like automaton, about to devour her.

G-Mamma faced her group of clones. 'Get your father out of here, Blonde,' she cried, using her SuSPInder as a lasso. Unfortunately her carbon copies were all doing the same – any moment now G-Mamma would be decapitated by a flying spy belt from the chanting, wiggling G-Mamma clones, who stopped every so often to form a cheerleader pyramid former and toss one of their number back to the floor in a spinning ball of fuchsia:

'Don't ya wish that you had fled? Or had just stayed in your bed?

Cos you're gonna lose your head, And you'll really be so dead!'

'That's rubbish!' yelled G-Mamma, body-rolling to the left to avoid a flying clone. 'My raps are way better than that! Blondette, do something!'

'I can't!' Janey was powerless to help, overwhelmed by the bunch of Janey Browns and the huge battalion of Jane Blondes advancing upon her, the first with their head on one side and their hair in their eyes in a wave of wimpiness that threatened to drown them all, the second forming their white-blonde ponytails into forward-facing daggers, ready to stab, stab, stab as they dropped their heads towards Janey.

'We're trapped,' whispered Janey in horror. They were all pinned against the trailer containing Bert, Jean and Abe.

Bert was still shaking, but now it seemed to be with hysterical laughter. 'Look at us,' he said, unable to wipe his, which were pouring with mirth. 'We're like one of those crime teams. The Dubbo Seven! Apart from we aren't any flaming use.'

'Speak for yourself, Sheep Dude,' snapped G-Mamma. 'We're lots of use. Just . . . just not against this many of them. Of us. Of those . . . things.'

The creeping fingers were just reaching out to close around their throats. Janey gagged as her Janey Brown mirror image, a Chloe, cocked her head on one side as she pressed a finger into her neck just below her ear. 'Sorry, Janey. Really sorry.'

'Stop saying sorry!' she tried to scream, but the air was being squeezed out of her, and as she struggled, writhing this way and that, she could see that every one of her friends was in the same boat, powerless against the multitudes of clones. They were done for. Nothing short of a miracle was going to save them now.

And maybe that's what it was, she thought, as her eyes stared up at the unbroken blue of the sky above the Spy-clone, and something white – glowing and white – swept across her vision.

An angel, she thought. My angel. And my . . . my cat?

.

Chapter 22 Spy-plane

G et the . . . What the devil is that?' cried the Abe-clone.

The other clones looked up. The thing above their head was too big a distraction to ignore. And anyway, it was shooting at them.

Cries of alarm and pain crackled around the Spylab as clone after clone was shot in the eye, the shoulder, the foot by the marauding gunner flying above their heads, and pretty soon the whole assembled army was cowering under fire, crouching low to avoid the vicious pellets.

'He's got a point,' said Bert amiably. 'What *is* that?'

As the clones clutched at each other and tried to hide from the aerial onslaught, Janey realised that none of the bullets was coming in their direction. Whoever was flying the little white plane was clearly on their side and was avoiding firing at them. She dared to look up again and her jaw dropped as it dawned on her what was swooping around above their heads. When she realised too what the bullets were, she closed her mouth very quickly.

'Maddy,' she said breathlessly, starting to laugh. 'It's Maddy! She's been through the Wower! Look, that's Trouble on her back, steering. He must have shown her what to do. Ha!' she screamed to the heavens, watching her favourite sheep loop the loop before targeting the Abe-clone in the centre of the army and moving in for a singular and prolonged attack. 'Not so ugly now, is she?'

'That's my girl,' cried Bert, while G-Mamma whooped and clapped, yelling a quickly improvised rap. 'Listen to this one, you sloppy copies!

That Maddy's not too baddy
She is really not too shabby
Our favourite ugly sheep!
The one we want to keep . . . Now that's a rap!'

'That's a sheep?' Alfie shoved at the nearest Alfie-clone, who was teetering around with his hands over his eyes, and was rewarded with a domino-fall of Alfies that tumbled against the ranks of Mrs Hallidays, who collapsed into the G-Mammas and Jeans until the whole room was toppling over in neat, serried ranks. 'It's more like a Spit-fire.'

'Hard to believe,' said Janey with a grin.

Maddy was magnificent. Her bald patch was a gleaming shellac pilot seat on which Trouble now perched, pulling Maddy's elongated ears this way and that to steer her in the right direction. Her cotton-wool puff of a tail was pert and upright, sleek as a rudder, but most miraculous of all was what had happened to the matted flaps of wool that had previously hung sadly from around her bald patch. The Wower had woven them into silken, flowing wings that streamed out on either side of her, exactly like the angel

Janey had taken Maddy for when she first saw her flitting gracefully across the open circle of light above the Spy-clone cone.

She was indeed a winged beauty, as glossy and glowing as any cloned sheep, and a million times more useful, especially with a ready supply of hard little sheep-poo pellets to fire at anyone who crossed her path.

Maddy was making mincemeat of the Abe-clone.

The number of times he had called her names, used her for his experiments and stripped her of her natural good looks clearly rankled so much that she now hated him fervently. Trouble too was no fan of the clone, and the pair of them were taking great delight in circling the tall figure, shooting at him from very close quarters and swiping at him with Maddy's cloven hooves. Suddenly they were close enough for Trouble to attack, and with a flick he leaned forward and embedded his sabre- claw in the Abe-clone's neck. The scream of pain was horrifying; Janey thought for a moment that Trouble must have caught a major vein, the jugular perhaps. Maybe the Abe-clone was dying!

But the scarlet gash was at the back of the neck, not on the side. The Abe-clone wheeled around, arms flaying as he tried to unseat the flying cat and knock Maddy to the ground. 'On your feet,' he bellowed, raging with fury and pain. 'My neck – again! Aargh – my neck! On your feet!' He scurried hither and thither, pulling clones up to a standing position and smacking them viciously into line, his eyes alight with an insane fury. 'Kill them! Kill them all – except the boy. Kill those SPIs!'

'What did I ever see in that man?' said Jean with a curl of lips. She looked round at Abe's prone body in the trailer beside her. 'Or is it that man? Anyway, time to wake up now, Jean. Wake up. Wake up before the dream man kills you.'

'Oh no.' Janey started to breathe faster, looking around as the clones stumbled to their feet and recommenced their terrible advance, reaching again for their spy weapons or curling their fists, intent on killing every single one of them except, for some reason, Alfie. Her ponytail whipped from side to side as she took in the Boy-battlers about to pound into Alfie's body to quieten but not kill him, the fearsome teeth poised to tear Mrs Halliday to shreds, the whistling SuSPInders looping towards G-Mamma's throat, catching at her fair bubbly curls and whisking through them like a razor so that the air around her was misty with chopped hair. Janey was filled with horror, not because the clones were now licensed to kill, but because a terrible truth had just been revealed to her . . .

'Alfie . . .' she said under her breath. 'Alfie, you have to help. Save us . . .'

'Wh -what?' Alfie turned to her, too confused to move. 'How can I save you?'

Janey could barely say the words. 'The Abe-clone – moaning about his neck "again'. Wanting to save you, and you only. It isn't a clone at all. It's a real person, Crystal Clarified.'

'Like your dad did?' Alfie swiped at a Mrs Halliday clone that was attacking his mother.

'Like *your* dad did, too,' said Janey grimly. 'Fake Abe – he's Copernicus.'

Chapter 23 A satispying result

'No way.' Alfie's face took on the slightly green tinge that overcame him whenever his father was mentioned.

It was not good news. The very thought of it made Janey shudder. Copernicus disguising himself as her father and creating cloned armies of minions. What on earth would he be able to do next? She assumed that this also meant that he had been able to find out her father's every move – whatever discoveries her dad had made, it was probable that Copernicus now knew about them: the Crystal Clarification Process, through which one creature could be transformed into another; the cat's-nine-lives secret – whoever knew about that was more or less immortal; and now the duplication of the creatures – rooms full of them, farms full of them, even whole countries full of them. If nobody stopped him, he could take over the . . . the world. The only thing he hadn't known about was how Janey had travelled to Dubbo Seven, and now he knew that too.

'He'll save you and not us – it makes sense. And now I think about it,' gasped Janey, high-kicking a Blonde clone and spinning round to take on another, 'he's been sounding very cold, very . . . you know . . . Copernicus.'

G-Mamma leaped over to Janey's side, punching a rapping G-Mamma-clone in the mouth and corralling another six together with her SuSPInder. 'You reckon that's old Copper Knickers himself? Explains a lot – particularly why your dad must have realised you were in mortal danger and whizzed himself over here.'

Janey glanced over at her father. Colour was seeping back into his face, but he still looked kitten-weak, and not at all able to help them. The clones were all around them. For each one she felled with her karate moves or her SPI-buys, there would be another to take its place, another with the sole mission of snuffing out her life. The others were too taken up fighting off their own clones, and her parents and Bert were not even able to retaliate. So far the clones hadn't reached them, crouched in their trailer behind the frontline defence of Blonde, G- Mamma and the two Halos, but it was only a matter of time before Janey and team were overwhelmed.

'Alfie!' Janey gripped his arm to get his attention.

'Busy here, Blonde,' he said abruptly, elbowing a clone of himself in the sternum to avoid the swinging Boy Battler that was directed at his ear.

'I know, but you're just going to have to promise – you know we can't win this. They'll overpower us, there're so many of them. And Mum and Bert and Dad can't even fight back. Promise you'll stop your father doing . . . whatever it is he plans to do.'

Alfie stopped short and looked hard at the floor for a few moments. Then he spat on his free hand and reached over to shake on it. 'If it kills me too,' he said seriously. 'That's a spy promise.'

Janey could feel death edging nearer in an evil tide. Outnumbered, out-spied.

Her only thought as the blank, terrifying faces of the clones gathered in a mighty crowd in front of them, with Copernicus screaming from the back, 'Move on! NOW! Save the boy!' was to say goodbye to her parents. She booted a G-Mamma clone out of the way and turned to the trailer.

Picking up her dad's hand, she felt with a horrible sense of irony that his pulse was stronger now. She kissed his palm and held it to her cheek for an instant. 'Bye, Dad,' she whispered. 'And I'm . . .' She'd been about to say she was sorry, but the image of Chloe and her constant apologies filled her mind so she changed tack quickly. 'I'm really proud to have been your daughter.'

She ran around to hug her mother, feeling once again that some strange hard object was behind her mum's back. 'You're the best mum in the world,' said Janey, fighting back tears.

'Thank you,' said Jean. 'And I'll make you a great breakfast just as soon as I wake up. I don't understand it – I keep opening my eyes and it's broad daylight.'

Janey squeezed her mother tighter, looking up at the sun pouring through the hole in the roof. It was directly overhead, she noticed. Noon. High noon. And Jean still thought she could just wake up from this nightmare and it

198

would all be OK. Janey's hand brushed against the object behind her mother again, and suddenly her mouth went dry.

She gulped. Maybe it could be OK. She had nanoseconds in which to execute a dramatic plan to save them all, but she was, after all, Jane Blonde.

'Good at spying, chewing gum, and . . . and boomerang throwing,' she said aloud, pulling the hard shape out from between her mother and Bert.

'Eh, don't go losing that,' he said, then looked around at the killer crowd around him. 'Ah, what the heck. Do your worst.'

'I'll do my best,' said Janey firmly, her heart racing with hope. 'G-Mamma, SPInamite!'

Her SPI:KE held off a clone with a roller-skated foot, and threw the chewed sweet to Janey. 'No blowing us up!'

'Don't worry, it's not for that.' It was still moist and stretchy. 'Perfect,' she said as she stuck it firmly on to the boomerang. Then, with all the volume she could muster, she yelled, 'SPIs, keep well back!' as she slid her USSR off her finger and on to the wad of SPInamite, so that it was anchored to the wood as if set in concrete.

She pushed the diamond once, drew back her arm, and flung the boomerang out across the Spylab.

It seemed to go in slow motion. All heads turned as it arced up and to the left, narrowly missing the noses of G-Mamma and Alfie as they watched it *whump- whump- whump* its way in a vast circle, over to the platform and

199

the door leading out to the SPIral, round behind the Spy-clone and past the Spylab doorway. It could only have been moments, but it felt as if they all stood, frozen in time, for hours, until the boomerang whirled past Trouble and Maddy who were floating near Janey, swooped down in front of the trailer, and landed neatly back in Janey's hand. The air vibrated all around them.

'So hang on. You've whizzed the USSR right around them, and now they're all . . . *inside* a force field?' G-Mamma shrugged at Janey. 'It's supposed to protect us, not them.'

'It has! Please have worked,' Janey said under her breath, reaching into the trailer for her father's fingers again. She lifted his hand up above the wooden side of the trailer, pointed it at the huge USSR force field she had created, and pressed firmly on the central button of the Satispy remote control.

'You're not sending us up on that death trap of a satellite thing?' Alfie had long distrusted the Satispy, a piece of SPI technology that allowed humans to be transported in a stream of cells up to a satellite dish in space and then be zapped down to their chosen destination in another part of the world.

'Not us,' said Janey. 'Them.'

There was a moment in which nothing happened, in which Janey's stomach felt as though it were going to burst out of her insides, and the shocked faces of the clones and Copernicus within the force field turned to triumph.

Several of the G-Mamma clones gurned madly and joined hands, intending to flip a clone right at Real G-Mamma, and fifty sets of lips slid back to expose some vile pointed teeth.

In an instant the Spylab turned blue. The clones, vacant expressions disintegrated into cellular soup as they shot off, mingling and disintegrating, towards the Satispy satellite. They had a journey through space of several thousand miles ahead of them. A deafening hum erupted from the force field, knocking the SPIs off their feet; Janey found herself sitting in the trailer on top of her father's feet, and Maddy and Trouble tumbled from the air down on top of her.

Then suddenly Alfie was cheering, laughing, and pulling at her shoulders.

'It worked! For once the stupid thing worked!' Not surprisingly, he hadn't forgotten the time he and Janey had SatiSPIed together and swapped hands and voices mid-flight.

Suddenly Janey's father stirred. 'That earthquake . . . was it an earthquake? It woke me up.'

G-Mamma whooped deliriously. 'Earthquake? It was a Blonde-quake! Your girl just sent a kazillion bony clonies all by Satispy. Yee hah!'

'Ah,' said her father thoughtfully, blinking the sleep from his eyes. 'I'm not sure that's a great idea. They might all be mixed up, and not very well, but you'll just have lots of mutated clones roaming around your Spylab, G-

Mamma. That's where I travelled from when you didn't get to me at the South Pole and I realised my messages had you racing off here, right into danger.'

'No, it'll be fine! There won't be any clones left.' Janey grinned confidently. 'It's one puzzle that nobody could work out, not even me. But I've just used it to our advantage. Come on, let's get to the SPIral staircase.'

They made their way across to the high door to the platform. As they reached the top of the stairs, Janey thought of something. 'The South Pole? That's where you were?'

Her father nodded. 'I sent you directions. Thought you'd get it: a circle around the southernmost tip on the compass. But I had to do it in a bit of a hurry as Copernicus's goons were after me. Sorry if it wasn't –' He paused for breath – 'wasn't very clear.'

'I should have known,' said Janey, shaking her head. 'You wouldn't send me half a clue.'

'I've sent you half a dad,' her father replied wryly. 'And a whole lot of trouble.'

'We'll be fine,' said Janey with a grin. 'Into the SPIral. We'll go in relays. Bert, you might want to stay here . . .'

'No chance,' said the farmer with an even broader grin. 'This is even more fun than the sheep-shearing regional finals.'

'Squeeze in with me. Hallidays first, then the Browns, and then, you know, us.' G-Mamma was eyeing Bert as if

202

he was a piece of cake, and with a quick glance to check she wouldn't bite or rap like her clones, Bert nodded.

'I could just go and get some Lamingtons for the journey,' he said.

G-Mamma's smile broadened even further. 'Lamingtons? They're not little sheep, are they? They're food? Excellent.'

'See you there,' said Janey, and she took her eSPIdrills and the SPIFFIG from the Spylab bench. She'd make this journey on her own, back through the centre of the Earth.

Chapter 24 Wower power

Janey corkscrewed through the Earth at lightning, hardly able to take in her blurred surroundings but now recognizing the pull as she reached through the Earth's core. She grinned as she stamped her Fleet feet to spur her on through the amazing purple steely glow at the epicentre of the planet. Definitely metal, she thought. When she arrived in G-Mamma's garden, the SPIFFIG's helmet was completely obscured by a grey mist made up of a fine metal fuzz, like the iron filings in her magnetic experiments kit.

Heaving herself out of the hole at G-Mamma's, she wiped a clear space on the SPIFFIG helmet and smiled up at the moon. It was the dead of night here, cool and still – exactly as Janey had planned once she'd realised that the midday sun was directly overhead in Australia. Everything seemed very quiet. She pulled the SPIFFIG off and stepped through G- Mamma's door, being careful to keep to the edges of the SPIral steps in the case the lift capsule suddenly appeared.

A dripping sound caught her ear. '

Ye-url,' said Janey, pulling a face.

Above her head was the hole in which the capsule would stand; right at this moment it looked like the inside of a monster's mouth. Viscous goo stretched in great snotty stalactites from its rim, pooling in a disgusting sticky puddle around Janey's feet and oozing out towards the garden. Janey wiped   the worst of it off her soles against the skirting board, then activated her Fleet-feet jump and bounced straight into G-Mamma's Spylab . . . she found herself knee deep in slime.

'Gaa, disgusting,' she moaned, then waded over to the Wower. At least that had its door closed, so it wouldn't have been invaded by the melted clones.

Janey smiled to herself as she trudged past G-mamma's fridge, hoping that no clones had been SATISPIed in among the doughnuts. It had been a bit of a gamble, but it had paid off. She had used the Cinderella effect to her advantage. Knowing that cloned sheep didn't survive beyond sundown, she had brought sunset on a little earlier than usual for the spy- clones and they clones all melted into sicky little sticky pools.

For the first time Janey felt almost smug. She had really been rather brilliant. Not only had she demoed her superb boomerang skills to an admiring audience, but she had actually saved that same audience from certain death.

'Go, Blondey! Go Blondey!' she chanted happily as she threw open the Wower door. 'Go . . . aargh!'

A reptilian arm, more tentacle than human limb, suddenly gripped her by the ankle and dragged her, screaming pointlessly and unheard, into the cubicle. She had been absolutely right about all the clones, but she had forgotten one very important detail – one of them was not a clone at all. It was a Crystal-Clarified person, who would not be affected by the Cinderella effect.

Copernicus.

'I should just twist your stupid Blonde head off your skinny shoulders,' rasped a hideous voice from deep within the vile creature.

Janey hardly dared to look, remembering only too well what had happened to Alfie and her when they'd SatiSPIed together.

'You've caused me so much aggravation, Spylet. Just like your father.'

She turned her head slowly, and very nearly threw up. The Satispy had ravaged Copernicus's body, but then he must have tried to strengthen himself by using the Wower. It had magnified all his most monstrous elements of him and now he hung, half-person, half-squid, from the mirrored wall of the Wower. The Abe-Clarification had been pared away on the Satispy journey, exposing raw sinew and gore under a grossly enlarged skull, the jaw held on only by the ropes of tendon that moved, snake-like, as Copernicus snarled demonically. Trouble's deep scratch on top of appallingly singed skin had opened a disgusting deep maw in the back of his neck, almost as if he had ripped open a second mouth.

And instead of the damaged, weakened legs of Copernicus or the long, lean arms of Abe Rownigan, there was now a writhing mass of four, five, six or more slithering, reaching, murderous limbs, neither arm nor leg, human nor creature. One of these had a tight grip around Janey's neck, and she closed her eyes against the stink and sight of the slime that oozed venomously over his entire body.

'You can't stop me, little Spylet,' seethed Copernicus, the words grating bubbling and sucking through mucus. 'You and your father are not going to get in my way again.'

'I think I just did!' Janey squeaked, hoping she sounded braver than she was feeling. Come back now, she begged silently. Come back now . . . She strained to hear the arrival of the SPIral staircase, and help, but the only sounds were the rumbling, slimy escape of bubbles from the atrocity that was Copernicus's mouth and her own short, jerky breathing.

'An interruption only.' The grip around her neck tightened, and suddenly Janey found that she was pinioned at the ankles as well.

'Well, go on then, kill me.' Waiting for death was harder than inviting it, she decided. At least if it came quickly, she wouldn't have to witness the demise of any of her friends or her family.

The hideous baggy squid head rocked from side to side before her. 'Unfortunately I still need you. Otherwise nothing would give me greater pleasure.'

'Need me for what?' Nothing, no matter what he envisaged, would tempt her to do anything Copernicus said, but any information about his plans might help her to thwart them. 'You know how to do the cloning. You've mastered life creation, immortality and duplication. What else can you want on top of that?'

At this, Copernicus threw back his monstrous head and emitted a horrible laugh, and Janey flinched at the sight of the inside of his throat pulsating and twitching. 'I'm ready to claim my rightful place as the Sun King, ruler of the planets.'

'What . . . how? You can't rule the Earth!'

'No? Well, perhaps you are right. Wait and see.' And again the vile giant squid with the half-human body squelched with bilious laughter. 'Unfortunately I can do nothing without a human body. So I will take yours.'

'No!' screamed Janey, squirming to try to evade the ever-tightening grasp. 'You can't have my body! I'll never obey you.'

'You have no choice,' he rasped, twisting his tentacles cruelly.

Just at that moment to her joy and relief, the Wower door opened, and the faces of the Hallidays appeared, one above the other. 'What are you hollering . . . oh my word,' said Alfie. The two of them stared in revulsion at the monster clutching Janey by the throat. 'That's not . . .?'

'Son,' said Copernicus, his voice even more nauseating as a note of affection crept in.

'No way.' Alfie shook his head vigorously, stepping back on to his mother's foot. 'I didn't like you when you were actually semi-human. Now you're just . . . just . . .'

His skin turned pale and his eyes hardened. 'Put Janey down.'

Copernicus paused. 'That is for you to decide, son,' he hissed at length. 'I can put her down, or I can kill her. It's your choice.'

'Really? That's a hard one. Put her down.' Alfie made no attempt to keep his disgust and hatred from dripping through his words.

There was a long silence, and then the half-mouth of Copernicus twisted in an evil version of a smile. 'Then you come with me in her place.'

'No!' Alfie, Mrs Halliday and Janey all yelled out at the same time.

'Forget it,' said Janey. 'Get out of here.'

Alfie was shaking, looking from Janey to the monster that was his father, and back at his mother. 'I . . . What do you mean, I come with you?'

'You can be my right-hand man. I need that, you see, now I have . . . no . . . HANDS!' Copernicus laughed bitterly. 'I can still become great. Very great. Come with me, Al Halo. We can be great together.'

'And,' said Alfie slowly, 'if I do you'll let Janey go?'

'Believe me, it repulses me even to touch her.' Copernicus shuddered so that Janey too was shaken from head to toe. 'She has cost me so much. But that ends now.'

Janey winced as his tentacle-like limb squeezed around her neck so hard that a ringing started in her ears.

Within seconds, however, she realised that the noise wasn't in her head. It was an actual sound – the SPIral staircase shooting up through the Earth this time bringing her parents to the Spylab. Her SPI:KE wouldn't be back for a while. What would she want her to do in this situation?

She thought back to her training session in the small hours of Good Friday. Was it really just a few days ago? Achilles heel, she remembered. It was almost laughable. This pustulous monster didn't even have heels. But there was more to it than that. It wasn't his *actual* heel that she needed to consider. It was his Achilles heel. His weakness. And all at once, she knew exactly what that was. There might just be a way out of this.

'You promised, Alfie,' she said suddenly, struggling to speak with a tentacle coiled around her throat.

'What?'

'You promised to save us. You spat on your hand and everything. You have to do it.'

The memory flitted across Alfie's face. He remembered that it was true, but he never could have imagined that this was the way he would have to keep his word.

'You go with your . . . father, and I get to go free. You promised.'

Alfie was dumbstruck, looked as though he might even cry, but his mother caught the wild look in Janey's eye and slowly nodded too. 'I heard you promise, Halo,' she said softly. 'You have to. It will break my heart, but you have to.'

'Always were sickeningly honourable, weren't you, Maisie,' scoffed Copernicus.

And Alfie stiffened. It was his weakness too, Janey realised: just how much he hated his father. He would do anything to stop him belittling his mother. He stepped up to the Wower door.

'Honour is a family trait,' Alfie said firmly. 'Our side of the family, not yours, sicko,' he added venomously. Then he turned to his mother and clasped an arm around her shoulders to say goodbye.

Janey noticed the grip on her own neck was loosening. She reached an arm out to the wall to steady herself, then waited for Copernicus to drop her to the floor. It seemed to take forever, but finally he loosened the agonising fleshy circlets around her neck and legs.

The second he did, she directed the laser finger of her Girl-gauntlet at the small sticky blob she had just attached to the inside of the Wower.

The huge, weighty head of Copernicus couldn't turn quickly enough to see what she was doing; in moments, she had crouched on the floor, body-rolled out into the Spylab and slammed the Wower door shut with her feet. 'Get back!' she yelled, bracing her Fleet-feet against the Wower . . .

The explosion rocked the whole of the Spylab and, Janey expected, most of her house next door as well. The

211

entire Wower cubicle e rose several feet off the floor as the sides imploded with the blast. Janey was thrown back against the computer bench, her head ringing once again with the sound of SPInamite going off inside the Wower.

The Halos stared, blinking, at the warped Wower, then clambered to their feet.

'Quick thinking,' said Alfie, offering her a hand. 'I honestly thought you meant it for a moment.'

'As if,' said Janey. 'Now, are you sure you want to see this?' Janey crossed to the misshapen lump of metal that used to be the Wower. 'It is your dad, after all.'

'That was some evil creature from the deep,' said Alfie. 'Nothing to do with me.'

Janey opened the door just as her parents stepped into the Spylab. Her father crossed to her side, and together she, Abe and Alfie peered into the Wower. There was very little left to see. Only a few coagulated lumps of flesh remained; Janey turned on the shower head and rinsed them away down the drain.

'He's gone,' she said firmly. 'Which is a good thing. I think he was on about ruling the world or something.'

Her father nodded. 'It wouldn't surprise me. He's mad enough to have had big plans afoot.'

'I think that would have to be "a-tentacle" – No feet,' offered Alfie. He looked rather pale, but Janey was glad to see that he could joke about it already.

Jean picked her way through the slimy lumps on the floor of the Spylab. 'Janey, you're here. I think I'm nearly home. Isn't that when I wake up? Please let me wake up. Although,' she said, turning to Abe, 'I must say it's very nice to see you again.'

'You too,' said Abe with a soft smile. 'All of you. It's very good to see all of you again. I'm still pretty weak though.'

'You'd better come and use our Wower.' Mrs Halliday pointed to the wrecked cubicle. 'Not much hope of getting that sorted out just yet.'

Abe put an arm across Janey's shoulders, and the other around Jean. 'Do you know, I think I might just have a bath. And something nice to eat.'

'Fish and chips?' said Janey.

Her father nodded and hit the fireplace button.

Chapter 25 Spy-days and holidays

Janey helped herself to some more apple crumble. 'So promise me you never intended to leave the spying world and close down Solomon's Polifficational Investigations.'

'One day I will, I hope,' said Abe. 'But while there are still people like Copernicus around, I daren't risk it.'

The new, top-of-the-range Wower was installed at G-Mamma's within a day, all organised by Janey's dad. This one had the ability to spin on its axis so that it became a horizontal room with a massage table in the middle, the Wower jets providing a powerful pounding to soothe the most rigid muscles. 'Just install a pizza oven and it'll be perfect,' suggested G-Mamma.

'That should last until the next modification. Sometimes it's very handy being the head of a spy organisation,' he said to Janey as Jean Brown, still complaining of a nasty headache, left the dinner table for water and a couple of aspirin. Days of being spied and de-spied, Wowed and de-Wowed, and hurtled through the very centre of the globe had done very little for her migraines, although she was completely unaware of their adventures and simply thought she'd been having some odd, feverish dreams.

'But he's not around any more!'

'Hopefully not,' said Abe. 'But don't forget he managed to get backs from the deep freeze, and nobody thought that would be possible.'

Janey nodded solemnly. 'He'd injected himself with tracer cells.'

'And the guards at the South Pole didn't realise that. Stupid of me not to think of it. See, I'll always have to keep one step ahead of him, instead of the other way round. He achieved cloning before I did, even though I was already working on it.'

Janey blushed. 'I thought I had a twin. I believed everything they said.'

'And why wouldn't you?' said her father. 'It's part of what makes you uniquely "you". You're very nice, and you can't imagine how horrible some people can be. I wouldn't swap you for the world.' And he flashed his real-life movie-star grin at her.

To their relief, Jean retired to bed early in the hope that a good night's sleep would get rid of her bad head once and for all. Abe and Janey slipped through to the Spylab for the grand unveiling of the Wower. Alfie and Mrs Halliday were bickering amiably over the crudités, and Janey was delighted to see Bert there, formally dressed in a white shirt, bow tie, jeans and a leather hat.

'Brought you something,' said Bert, nodding to Janey. He held out one of his enormous shovels of a hand, and there, curled up along his arm, was Trouble.

'Twubs!' she cried delightedly, rubbing her Spycat's quiffed head. 'You're back! Thanks. Er, what about Maddy?' she asked Bert.

'She always was my favourite,' said Bert. 'I'd like to keep her at the farm, if that's all right with you. No cloning or anything, but I might let her have the odd Wower.' He grinned at Janey, and then over her head at G-Mamma.

'Right,' said Janey's SPI:KE, fumbling in a drawer, 'and if any of your customers need silky-haired sheep, we'll do it the old-fashioned way.' She brandished a set of straightening irons, last used to smooth Trouble's fur.

'But . . .' Janey glanced at her father, who wore an amused expression, 'Bert, you're not a spy.'

At this, Abe strode over to Bert and reached for his hand. 'I don't know about that, Janey. I think Bert would be a very fine spy. I've never known anyone keep so cheerful and so quiet during such very strange times. I know you already feel you did some deals with me, but that was my doppelganger, Bert,' he said earnestly. 'I'm really not the same person. I'd be very honoured if you'd consider joining Solomon's Polifical Investigations and becoming a SPI yourself. You could be my Australian agent.'

Bert beamed as he pumped Abe's hand up and down. 'Delighted, mate,' he said eventually. 'As long as it means all me sheep can baa their own note.'

'Deal,' agreed Abe. 'Now, we'll have to give you a spy name.'

216

'Well, if it's all right with you,' said Bert, staring nonchalantly at the ceiling, 'I'll stick with Dubbo Seven. Saves me changing the gates and everything.'

Janey laughed, along with everyone else. It was cool, she decided, having this funny family of disappearing spies, friends with different identities and a father who was the head of his own spy group. She waved off the Hallidays, said goodbye to G-Mamma and Bert as they headed off to the SPIral staircase to sort out the next sheep contract in Dubbo and then walked with her father to G-Mamma's back door. Somehow she knew what was coming. And somehow, she was OK with it. For now.

'I'd better get back to headquarters and check everything's OK, now that I'm feeling better,' said Abe, dropping a kiss on Janey's forehead. 'Somehow I doubt that it is! Look after your mum for me, Blonde.'

'I will.' Janey threw her arms around Abe. 'Dad,' she added, with a little smile.

Janey leaned on the doorpost and watched him disappear off in the taxi. 'I think that after everything that's just happened, I might just take the train,' he'd said with a smile.

Janey agreed with him and, anyway, G-Mamma was right: it was pretty disgusting watching your family disintegrate before your eyes.

But her family were made of stern stuff, and she knew her father would survive all this. They were spying stock, after all.

217

And meanwhile, she thought as she slid through the fireplace tunnel on her ASPIC, there was still over a week of the Easter holidays to go. She was pretty sure her mum would enjoy what she and Abe had planned: a little getaway, just for the two of them.

In a cottage, in Wales.

THE END

ABOUT THE AUTHOR

Jill Marshall is a proud mum, nana and communications consultant, as well as the author of dozens of books for children, young adults and (old) adults. When she's not doing any of those things, she loves singing, dancing and theatre and going to see other people do singing, dancing and theatre. She divides her time between the UK and New Zealand, and hopes one day to travel between the two by SatiSPI.

Read the whole Jane Blonde series:
Jane Blonde Sensational Spylet
Jane Blonde Spies Trouble
Jane Blonde Twice the Spylet
Jane Blonde Spylet on Ice
Jane Blonde Goldenspy
Jane Blonde Spy in the Sky
Jane Blonde Spylets are Forever

Also featuring Jane Blonde–

S*W*A*G*G 1, Spook

OUT NOW!

Want the full SWAGG experience?

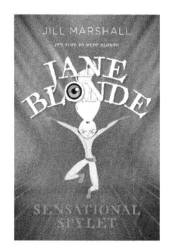

Immerse yourself in the origin stories.

The Jane Blonde series
Jane Blonde, Sensational Spylet
Jane Blonde Spies Trouble
Jane Blonde, Twice the Spylet
Jane Blonde, Spylet on Ice
Jane Blonde, Goldenspy
Jane Blonde, Spy in the Sky
Jane Blonde, Spylets are Forever

Jack BC in the Doghead trilogy
1 Jack BC, Doghead
2. Jack BC, Dogfight
3. Jack BC, Dogstar

The Legend of Matilda Peppercorn
TLOMP, Witch Hunter
TLOMP, Toadstone
TLOMP, Questioner
TLOMP, Trinity

Stein & Frank: Battle of the Undead People-Eaters

Also by Jill Marshall

Available in print, mobi, epub and audio.

For Young Adults
Pineapple
Fanmail
Lena's Fortune

For Adults
The Most Beautiful Man in the World
The Two Miss Parsons
As It Is on Telly

For younger children
Kave-Tina Rox

For more adventures and
information,

visit www.jillmarshallbooks.com

Follow Jill Marshall Books
on Facebook

Email jill on
info@jillmarshallbooks.com

Printed in Great Britain
by Amazon

36567310R00131